FREAK OF NATURE

JULIA CRANE

Freak of Nature
Copyright 2013 by Julia Crane

Published by Valknut Press
Clarksville, TN

First print edition, January 2013
ISBN 10: 162411024X
ISBN 13: 978-1-62411-024-5

"Freak of Nature" edited by Sarah Billington and Claire Teter
Cover art by Eden Crane Design
Formatted by Heather Adkins | CyberWitch Press, LLC

*Kaitlyn, Quess and Christine,
you know who you are!
Thanks for all your support.*

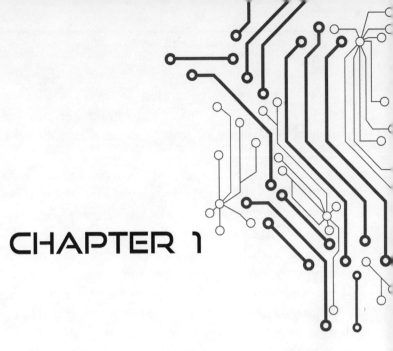

CHAPTER 1

Kaitlyn turned a corner and caught a glimpse of herself in a mirror. Seventeen years old. Long dark hair, grey eyes. At least her face hadn't been marred by the accident, or the upgrades since.

The rest of her body had not been so lucky.

Half-human, half-machine. She didn't quite fit into either world. I'm an abomination, she thought, her shoulders slumping. She tore her eyes away from her reflection in the mirror and continued to trudge down the stark hallway.

The only sound was the squeaking of her sneakers on the tiles. Everything—the walls, the cold tiles underfoot, even the trash cans—was sterile and white. If she never saw a white wall again, it would be too soon. The harsh lighting of the corridor often reminded her of a different bright light, the one that had ended her human life and began this stage of ... existence, if it could be called that.

After they brought her back from the brink of death, the IFICS staff told her she should be grateful. But they didn't know what it was like being prodded and probed, having no future and no past. If only she hadn't checked the "donate body to science" option on her driver's license, then she wouldn't have been in this situation. Although, if it weren't for IFICS—she still didn't know what the acronym stood for—she would probably be dead. Sometimes, she wondered which was worse.

At least she no longer needed an escort to get to the treatment room. That had been annoying, considering they'd replaced a section of her brain with a computer that learned far faster than any human's. In the early days while her new body acclimated with the machinery, her weakness made it necessary for her to rely on them for everything. It had humiliated her.

Footsteps echoed in the distance behind her. Her sensors kicked in, analyzing the sound of the steps and the length of the stride. She knew who it was before she heard his voice, and she waited for his familiar greeting.

"Kaitlyn." Lucas greeted her the same way he did every morning.

"Lucas."

If she still had a real heart, it surely would have skipped a beat or two. Lucas was the only thing in her crazy world that made getting out of bed worthwhile. He made her feel when the Professor and his team said it wasn't possible. At least, she thought it was feelings, and not just electrical charges pulsing through her system. But isn't that what happens in the human body, anyway? Kaitlyn reminded herself. Human emotions and reactions were nothing more than synapses firing, telling the brain what to do. For Kaitlyn, though, they weren't as strong anymore — the ghosts of feelings, just beyond her reach. But she knew they were there, and she knew she had them for Lucas — good feelings.

She fell into step beside him in the white corridor without another word. A part of her longed to connect with him, but fear kept her quiet. She had overheard enough to know if it became known that she still had thoughts and feelings of her own, they would quickly be erased. Her only friend, Quess, had confirmed it. She guarded what was left of her mind too much to give it away, even if Lucas did make her body hum.

With a look to her left, Kaitlyn took in his beautiful profile. She could stare at his full sensual lips and strong jawbone for hours. He walked with a relaxed gait, his wrinkled white scrubs swishing in the relative stillness of the hallway. His muscular frame had lifted her off the floor more than once during the early days of the treatments, when she was trying to adjust to her new body. His unruly dark hair curled at the nape of his neck — she noticed he was in need of a haircut. She had an overwhelming, illogical urge to reach out and brush his hair out of his eye.

What would it feel like to have his big, steady hands trail down her body? His lips on her neck? If she no longer felt pain, could she feel pleasure? Her mind was always trying to make sense of the madness that raced through it.

Appalled at the too-human thoughts, Kaitlyn tore her eyes from his face and clasped her hands together in front of her.

Their relationship was clinical: she knew Lucas saw her as only an experiment and nothing more. He would probably be repulsed if he knew the thoughts that ran through her head when he was near. Even worse — what if he decided to reprogram her? Her only friend, Quess, had warned her to keep her thoughts to herself. The company wanted a robot, not a confused half-breed. She couldn't risk them taking away anything more from her. Not even for Lucas.

The large double doors loomed ahead. She wondered absently what they had in store for her today. She'd long since accepted that her new existence meant she was a science project.

Knowing what happened behind those doors didn't fill her with loathing and terror like it would a real human. It would if she still had the flight or fight response, but her sensors overrode any sign of acute stress immediately.

Maybe what she felt for Lucas was nothing more than a short circuit. She glanced at him as he opened one of the doors. A persistent, spreading short circuit.

As soon as they walked through the door, Professor Adams pushed back his chair from his desk and stood, knocking a file onto the floor. His wiry gray hair was disheveled as usual, and his small, round glasses were perched crookedly on the end of his bulbous nose.

Kaitlyn's sensors activated. The green screen in her right eye kicked into gear and the bulls-eye dot centered on Professor Adams. There was the usual ticking sound in her ear but in less than a second it stopped, and she had his diagnostics: Unarmed. Physically out of shape. Not a threat.

No one else was in the room; if so, her heat sensors would've warned her. There was just the hum of the computers and the distant whir of the lab refrigerator.

"Lucas, we've upgraded Kaitlyn's microprocessor again, so I want you to compare her scans to last week," he said, as if she wasn't even there. Glancing over the top of his glasses, Professor Adams handed the clipboard to Lucas.

He flipped through the pages, and then nodded at Adams. "No problem."

Kaitlyn stood completely still but fought the sudden urge to roll her eyes. She wasn't sure why she would want to roll her eyes. The movement held no meaning; the very idea made no sense to her, though some part of her felt like it should. Maybe an old habit from her previous life?

She made a mental note to ask Quess later. She helped fill in the gaps that Kaitlyn often experienced.

"Kaitlyn." Lucas's sky blue eyes met hers briefly, then flickered away just as fast. The look made the pace of her breathing quicken, despite the mechanisms that regulated her body functions. "Please, sit down so I can attach the monitors."

Wordlessly, Kaitlyn walked over to the stainless steel table and sat down on the white plastic chair with her back to Lucas. She stared straight ahead at the large double sink, sitting as still as a statue and willed herself not to react to his touch. They wanted a robot, so that was what she gave them.

For now.

Lucas pulled the tape off the back of the electrode and softly pressed the round pad to her temple. He was so close she could smell his aftershave: a mixture of sandalwood and cedar with a hint of rosemary. Scanning, she analyzed the scents, and a list of potential brands flooded her mind.

Her body tensed as Lucas reached around her to press the other pad to her left temple. For an instant, the nearness of his warm body and his arm around her made it hard to breathe. Why did he alone have this effect on her?

Finished placing the electrodes and completely unaffected by their encounter, Lucas turned on his heel and switched the machine on.

A pulse of current invaded Kaitlyn's brain, and she straightened up in her seat. It wasn't painful; it was more of an annoyance. Like a slight buzz between her temples. Maybe even a tickle. She found it somewhat interesting that the test never picked up on her body's awareness of Lucas. Obviously, the computers didn't know everything.

She sat still as the test ran. Lucas scribbled notes on his clipboard, his face lit by the blue screen of the computer.

The door to the lab swung open, and a nurse walked in with short, brisk steps. Her long brown hair was pulled up into a ponytail today. It made her look younger. Kaitlyn had seen this woman every morning for the last eighty-nine days, but they never spoke. The nurse barely looked at her. Kaitlyn didn't even know her name. Quess told her that the staff was forbidden to interact with her unless it was necessary for testing.

"Almost done." Lucas spoke to the nurse who waited off to the side, clutching her little basket filled with vials. A smile lit the pretty woman's face, and her cheeks turned bright pink. Lucas seemed oblivious to the affect he had on women.

A couple of minutes later, Lucas pulled the pads off Kaitlyn's head and clicked the machine off. There was no touching this time—thankfully.

The nurse swabbed Kaitlyn's arm with a cotton ball that reeked of strong alcohol, careful to only touch the skin. Two shots were administered, and then her blood was drawn.

Kaitlyn felt nothing. A computer chip implanted in her brain overrode the nerves that told her she was experiencing pain.

Sometimes when she was locked in her room alone, she wondered what pain felt like. She couldn't remember. They assured her it was a good thing that she couldn't recall her past life, or the accident that had brought her there. Easy for them to say. It wasn't their lives that were ripped away from them.

Once in a while, Kaitlyn had flashes of memories, sitting behind a piano, running in the woods, or floating in the water. She was always alone, but it was like watching someone else. She felt no more of a connection to those memories than she did to the plots of movies. Whatever life she had before was gone.

"Kaitlyn, I need you to come over here."

Lucas's voice filled the room.

She didn't tell the staff about the memories for fear that they would have them removed, just like she didn't tell Lucas that he alone made her feel human.

Without a thought, Kaitlyn rose to her feet and walked towards Lucas, who stood beside the treadmill. The machine part of her obeyed before she had time to consciously acknowledge his command.

She stepped onto the treadmill and waited as he adjusted the settings.

"You know the drill." He stepped back, writing on his ever present clipboard.

Kaitlyn settled into a steady rhythm, the sensation of her sneakers pounding on the rubber, relaxing. There was nothing to look at but lab equipment—wallboards covered in scrawled numbers, cabinets full-to-bursting with gadgets and notebooks. She watched the blinking red numbers of the treadmill slowly rise.

"I'm going to increase the speed," Lucas told her, his hand blocking the numbers as he hit the 'up' arrow. "If you need me to stop, yell."

Kaitlyn nodded, so he knew she comprehended. It was annoying, the way they talked to her like she was an idiot when they were the ones who put a computer in her brain. Although, she never gave them a reason to do otherwise.

She let her mind wander as they tried to push her to failure.

As she ran faster and faster, arms swinging, she thought of how they could take her heart and her memories, but a small part of her mind was still her own. Something they failed to calculate into their little experiments. All they discussed was her potential: how they could use her to their advantage. The logical side of her knew they'd never talk like that around her if they for one minute thought she could still think for herself.

It would have made her sick to her stomach. Only she couldn't get sick. Her stomach was now nothing but titanium gears and who knew what else.

No one asked her opinion after the accident, when her body wasn't salvageable and on the brink of death. Apparently, she'd opted to donate her body to science, though in hindsight, she couldn't imagine why. IFICS had seen an opportunity, and they had taken it. Now Kaitlyn was left to pay the price for their greed. Over and over again.

"Sir, it's reached maximum capacity," Lucas said, clearly impressed.

"Very good." A grin spread across Professor Adams's face. "She continues to exceed expectations. Soon, she will be ready. Dr. Harrington will be pleased with the news."

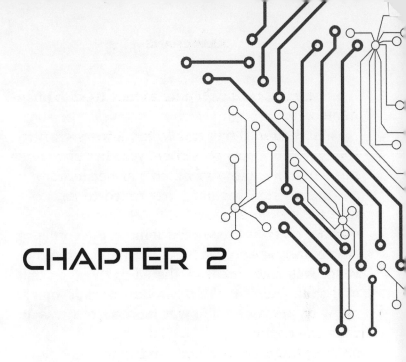

CHAPTER 2

Kaitlyn heard Quess plodding down the hall before she unlocked the door, and turned the doorknob. The poor girl had to spend her summers with her grandparents—Professor Adams and his wife. As punishment for some act of teenage belligerence, Quess had to clean this wing of the compound, which included Kaitlyn's room. Not that she minded, because it gave her more time with Quess.

Kaitlyn clicked off the television and leaned back on her pillow, her legs crossed in front of her at the ankles. She had already seen the movie Munich several times. She really enjoyed the movie, but welcomed the interruption. Recently, Professor Adams had a TV installed at Lucas's request. He thought she could learn about human interaction through watching movies. For some reason reality shows and the news were off-limits,which made no sense. Wouldn't she learn more from a reality show than make believe?

She peeked her head around the door. "Ms. Kaitlyn, may I come in?"

"Yes." The blinking red light in the corner of the room was an ever-present reminder that her room was monitored, so she had to watch what she said and did. That usually wasn't much, anyway. To say her life was monotonous was an understatement.

Quess dropped her bucket down on the floor, breaking the silence, and pulled out an old rag. She started dusting around Kaitlyn's room—not that there was much dust. The room was sparse. Kaitlyn watched as Quess's small pale hand efficiently wiped down the white dresser, and then moved over to the windowsill. Her unruly copper hair looked like fire in the sunlight.

Neither spoke a word. Kaitlyn wondered if the way she stared—robotic, silent, almost as if she were a statue—bothered Quess. Kaitlyn could sit for hours on end, unblinking and with nothing to do but stare at the four walls around her. But Quess never complained.

After Quess finished dry mopping the tile floor, she turned and looked at Kaitlyn with a mischievous glint in her hazel eyes. "Ms. Kaitlyn, would you like to walk the grounds with me? Grandpa Adams suggested you might want some fresh air."

Walking the grounds was Kaitlyn's favorite thing to do, but she kept her face stoic. She didn't want to show any emotions to the camera. They've already taken so much from her she wouldn't allow them to take anything more. "If Professor Adams thinks I need fresh air, then I will go."

"I thought you might." Quess picked up her bucket and waited for Kaitlyn to follow.

Anything to get out of this white, stuffy little room and away from the endless testing, Kaitlyn thought. She gracefully stood from her bed, smoothed down the front of her dress, and followed behind the young girl.

She remained silent throughout the maze of hallways, past the dark, quiet labs and the even darker cafeteria. Cameras were everywhere: posted in high, shadowed corners, hidden behind black-glass windows. Kaitlyn lived her entire new life—or half-life, as it were—under scrutiny, like the science experiment she was. Except on the rare occasion she went out with Quess. Even then they didn't have much privacy.

They stopped by the supply closet and stowed Quess's bucket before Kaitlyn pushed through the heavy metal door that led outside into the afternoon sunshine. The cool air against her skin was a nice sensation. Being locked away made her appreciate the little things.

Where the lab and dorm were sterile and white, outside was a mini paradise. Kaitlyn believed the compound was remote, being surrounded on all sides by thick forest and absent of any sounds beyond that of nature. A glance towards the distant front gate—hung with barbed wire and electronically locked—showed it was being patrolled by its usual armed guards.

Scanning the area, she was relieved to see the courtyard was empty as they made their way down the stone path flanked by dogwood trees leading to the woods. Sometimes staff members would sit at the picnic tables for lunch or dinner, or gather around the back door for a smoke break. Kaitlyn always felt awkward on the rare occasion she crossed paths with staff members who were not assigned to her. They either gawked at her like she was a freak or avoided eye contact completely.

Kaitlyn watched with curiosity as Quess spread her arms wide and twirled around laughing. Her head tilted up towards the sun.

"It's so beautiful." Quess gave one more twirl and linked her pale, skinny arm through Kaitlyn's.

Kaitlyn found human contact very strange. She could feel the warmth from Quess's touch, but she didn't understand why the girl would want to touch her. It made her uncomfortable.

She looked straight ahead and focused on putting one foot in front of the other. With her heightened sense of perception, she could hear wild life scurrying in the distance. A mother deer and her baby were grazing on the open field four hundred and twenty-two meters to their left. A persistent Pileated Woodpecker tapped away at a tree. Only a few feet away a squirrel jumped from one branch to another.

Once they passed the large birch tree—their normal point of safety from prying eyes—Kaitlyn looked at Quess and smiled dropping the mask she usually wore. There were only heat sensor cameras beyond this point in case anyone tried to break into the secure facility. The heat sensors made it possible for the guards to make the distinction between humans and animals.

"What did they do to you today?" Quess asked, her pretty freckled face tilted up to meet Kaitlyn's eyes.

Ever since Quess had warned her not to show any emotion around the staff, she'd considered the girl a companion. Kaitlyn shrugged. "Nothing interesting. More testing and physical activity." She remembered her stray thought about the 'rolling of eyes' and added, "But I do have a question for you."

"Sure." Quess slowed her pace.

"Quess, what does it mean for me to 'roll my eyes'? The phrase crossed my mind today at the oddest time. I felt like I should know what it meant, but I couldn't figure it out."

The young girl giggled. "It's so funny when you ask such strange questions. How can you remember you should wear pants, but not what rolling your eyes means?"

Kaitlyn sighed. "I wish I knew. My mind is a mess. I seem to only know what they *want* me to know. It's very frustrating."

"Well, that's where I can help out." Quess touched Kaitlyn's shoulder, a brief show of solidarity, or maybe, sympathy. "Rolling your eyes is just a saying. Well, really it's an action. Like if you think something is ridiculous, you roll your eyes. Watch." Quess came to a stop. She demonstrated, her hazel eyes making a full circle.

Kaitlyn thought about it for a moment, her mind categorizing not only the verbal definition but the visual. She grasped the meaning, but she couldn't understand why 'rolling of the eyes' had anything to do with it. She didn't bother to press the girl any further.

Who knew? A lot of sayings didn't make any sense to her logical, mechanical mind.

One time, Kaitlyn heard the professor say it was 'raining cats and dogs'. When she was relieved from the laboratory, she had rushed back to her room to look out the window. She wanted to see the animals falling from the sky, but there was nothing but a lot of rain.

Another time, she heard the Professor's wife tell him that he was 'going to hell in a hand basket,' because of his latest experiment. Even Quess didn't get the logic of that statement. The going to hell part made sense, but why in a hand basket? There were many mysteries in the english language.

"How much longer will you be here? Don't you start school soon?" Kaitlyn asked quietly. She hated the thought of being alone, and once Quess was gone, she really *would* be alone. No one else talked to her like she was a real person, like she was a human being. She was a machine to them. Just an experiment, with a more human-sounding project name than most.

"I'm staying here for school this year," Quess said. "Boarding school didn't agree with me."

Relief flooded Kaitlyn. She had been surprised that they would even let Quess near her, what with Kaitlyn's very existence being 'top secret.' Quess had explained that the professor and his team had used hypnosis on her; she would forget Kaitlyn whenever she stepped foot off the compound.

They'd thought of everything....

"What about your parents?"

Quess shrugged. "They don't care as long as my grades are good. It's not like they are ever around anyway. They are always traipsing around the world at some archaeological dig site or another."

Kaitlyn could tell the girl was upset, but had no idea what to say. Times like this she wished she were more human.

They walked in silence for a while.

"I heard some of the guards talking about you the other day."

Kaitlyn didn't care if she was talked about, but she knew that Quess enjoyed to gossip. So she tried to humor her when possible.

"What did they say?"

"Jimmy thinks your sexy and Terry says he would give his right arm for a fraction of your skills."

"His right arm?" Kaitlyn asked confused.

"It's just a saying. He wants to have your skills no matter what the cost."

"The cost is too high." Kaitlyn said sadly. She had often wondered if she were the only one Harrington had created.

"Are there any others like me?" Kaitlyn asked. Her eyes scanned her surroundings, the computer within checking over everything for potential threats as they walked.

Quess shook her head. "Not that I've seen. I think you're the only one. All of the other experiments I've seen have only been with machines. Not humans."

Kaitlyn had thought that was the case, but hearing it said out loud only made her loneliness that much deeper.

"I haven't been sleeping well." She wasn't sure why she told Quess, but it had been on her mind. Anything out of the norm always caught her attention.

"Have you had that dream again?" Quess looked up, her eyes wide.

Kaitlyn gazed across the green courtyard. The sun was setting in the distance, turning the sky a dozen different shades of red. "Every night that I can recall," she murmured.

"I wonder who the guy is. He must be important if you keep dreaming about him."

"I have no idea. Perhaps someone from my old life." A life she could not recall.

"Maybe we can find him," Quess said excitedly.

Kaitlyn laughed. Her friend was so young and human. "I don't think that is likely, Quess."

"You can describe him to me, and I can make a sketch, and we can run a search. I bet he has a Facebook account."

Kaitlyn had no idea what a 'Facebook account' was, but she did know she could describe the stranger's face, down to the small scar on his chin. Shaggy dirty blond hair, emerald green eyes, an infectious smile.

"If he even exists, he thinks I'm dead. Besides, *they* would see," Kaitlyn told her firmly, refusing to allow even the smallest bit of hope to emerge from her human side. "They see everything, Quess."

"Not everything," Quess cooed, skipping a few steps. "There are a few hidden spots that the cameras don't reach."

Kaitlyn stared down at the beautiful young girl. "And how do you know that?"

"I've been watching the gardeners."

"The gardeners? What do they have to do with anything?"

"Well, they always take their breaks at the same spot. Behind one of the large oak trees."

"So?" Without prompting, Kaitlyn's machine kicked in, offering an alternative explanation. Sometimes she hated that thing inside her, kicking out logical commands so that Kaitlyn hadn't a clue if the thought was even her own. "Maybe they just like to be in the shade."

"Kaitlyn, come on. You're the one that told me to look at the little details. How many trees are on this property? Countless, and yet *all three* gardeners rest in the *same place*. I've even seen one napping."

Kaitlyn grinned at her astute friend. "You're going to make a great spy someday."

"Maybe, or an artist. I haven't made up my mind," the fourteen-year-old said matter-of-factly.

"Where is this tree, and do you have paper and pencil on you?"

Quess walked backwards, smiling proudly as

she pulled a small notebook from the back pocket of her jeans. "An artist always has something to write on. Follow me."

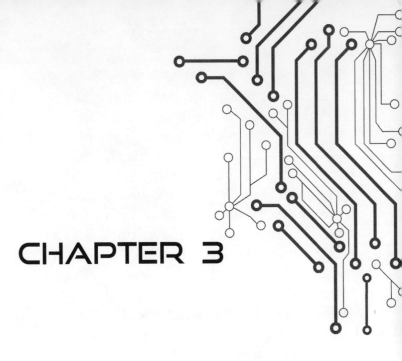

CHAPTER 3

Outside, the rain poured on a dreary early morning. It had taken everything in him just to get out of bed and come to work. He wanted to blame his foul mood on the weather, but he knew that wasn't it.

"Lower extremities fully functional," Lucas checked off the box. He pressed harder than he meant to, and his pen ripped across the paper, tearing a hole in the document. Sighing, he smoothed the ragged edges down.

Get a grip, he chided himself.

Looking up from his clipboard, Lucas sneaked another look at Kaitlyn. God, she was beautiful. Just one glance, and he felt weak in the knees. He tapped his pen on the page and willed his mind to get back on task. "Heart rate sixty." He jotted down the number.

She's a piece of machinery, no different from half the computers that fill this room. His thoughts made him feel sick to his stomach. What was wrong with him? He tossed the clipboard onto the desk.

There were days he wished he had never crossed paths with the master mind behind this project. His conscience had been bothering him more and more lately. The closer Kaitlyn got to completion, the more he questioned the morality of the project. Sure, it was astounding the way the human body could adapt to the merging of electronics, but still—the poor girl never gave her consent for this. When donating her body after death to science, well, more than likely, she would have thought she'd be dead. That fact alone told a lot about her personality. Not many seventeen year olds would even consider donating their body to science. But that was the type of person she is… or *was*.

"Kaitlyn, we need to go outside today," Lucas spoke into the stillness of the lab, his voice barely audible above the steady thrum of rain on the windows. "To make sure none of your hardware shorts in the rain with the new protective shields. We want to make sure they seal properly." For some reason Harrington insisted they change the clear covers for teal. It wasn't like she was going to color code her outfits to the mechanics.

"Okay." She didn't bother to look his way. She rarely looked at him. Of course she didn't— they had taken anything human about her and destroyed it.

He grabbed his keys off the edge of his desk.

Lucas was probably going to need a psychiatrist after this job. How had he even gotten himself into this madness? He knew exactly how—the eccentric billionaire, Dr. Harrington, who shared Lucas's obsession with electronics and science. His thesis on genetic mutation had caught the attention of Harrington. Cornell happened to be Harrington's Alma Mater, and as one of the largest contributors, he got tipped off to promising students that could be a match for IFICS.

Unlimited funds and cutting edge science. Lucas couldn't turn down an offer that had seemed so much like a dream come true. Just the thought had sent a shiver through him. He didn't even think twice about accepting.

But Lucas never dreamed that the job would entail taking a human's life away from her and making her into some kind of combat robot. If he were honest with himself, given the chance, he would accept again in a heartbeat. He hated himself for it.

"The track or obstacle course?" Kaitlyn asked, her voice monotone. It wasn't that she cared one way or another, he knew. She was scanning her hardware, preparing for what her body would need. That was how she was wired—know the challenge, meet it, succeed.

For a brief moment, their eyes met. Lucas had never heard her with emotion in her voice. How would she sound if she could feel happiness? Sadness? He would never know.

Lucas turned roughly, giving her his back but not an answer. He closed his eyes, and grabbed the discarded clipboard laying on the desk.

Why was he drawn to her? Every time he was near her, she sent him into a tailspin. He hadn't expected something meant to be a cutting edge science experiment to affect him. After all their time together, it should've worn off. He shouldn't still think of her as human. What did that say about him? Nothing good he was sure.

The guilt had not left him since she arrived. If anything, it had increased. She was a person. A human. A beautiful, living, helpless girl chosen to become Dr. Harrington's lab rat and have every ounce of her humanity erased. He wished he had known her *before* they altered her personality.

How many nights had he lost sleep searching through her old social media sites and reading the newspaper clippings? He had longed to know everything about the girl whose life they were going to alter in the name of science. It tore him apart seeing the person she once was come to life on his computer screen. She had been kind and adventurous, and there were hundreds of pictures of her with her friends. In her pictures, she looked much like she did now, with long dark hair that spilled over strong shoulders. But there was a big difference–she smiled. And it radiated real, true happiness. Her smile was contagious, her eyes bright and intelligent. He smiled at the thought of the image of her giving the thumbs-up before she dove from a plane. The same friends mourned her enough that they still kept a memorial page for her on Facebook. They still posted about the fun times they'd had.

They missed her because she was more than a body donated to science. And Lucas read every post.

The way she lost her life was tragic. But it was yet another example of the personality they took from her. She lost her life trying to save another.

Pull yourself together, Lucas warned himself. There was work to be done. He had to find a way to keep professionally detached. *Yeah right.*

Leave it to him to fall for the one girl who wouldn't—and couldn't—give him the time of day.

Enough already. Lucas shook his head. He was wasting time with his daydreams.

Standing up, he reached over the back of his chair and grabbed his jacket. The rain was really coming down. He should dose up on Vitamin C when he got home, to be safe. He couldn't afford to get sick. Not when they were so close to completion.

"We're going to the obstacle course," he finally answered.

When he turned back around to face her, he found she hadn't moved. Not even an inch. Her unflinching, impassive face just stared at him as he shrugged into his jacket. *What had they done?*

He longed to see something human from her, but all he got was that familiar blank stare. He wasn't sure why he hoped he'd one day see something different. It wasn't like she could think for herself or even feel. Not after all they had done to her. He missed the days before the upgrades. Early on, he'd wondered if she would be able to keep part of her personality, but it was soon obvious they had stripped any remaining spark out entirely.

They drove in silence deep into the woods. He longed to talk to her, but he had no idea what to say. A flash of lightning illuminated the sky filled with grey clouds. Lucas thought the whole thing was a horrible idea, but they needed to know if the elements would affect the project. They had already done a shower test, and she'd come through that fine, but they needed to see if the wind and rain would affect her abilities. If she shorted out, it would be a potential nightmare on a contract job. He zipped his jacket and jumped out of the Jeep, then rushed around to open Kaitlyn's door, but she had already exited the vehicle.

He hoped she didn't short circuit and get hurt. He felt a sudden urge to turn around and tell Professor Adams he wanted nothing to do with this craziness anymore. But doing so would mean leaving her to the Professor and Dr. Harrington. He couldn't do that. He felt this overwhelming need to protect her, which was ironic since he had played a huge part in turning her into a cyborg.

Frustrated, he ran his hands through his wet hair and glanced over at Kaitlyn. He watched for any sign that the weather was affecting her mechanics. She stood still and ready in nothing more than miniscule running shorts and a tank top. Sexy as hell.

She didn't appear bothered by the cold; all systems must have been working, her body adapting and regulating her temperature as needed. Lucas, on the other hand, was wet and freezing and longed to put his arms around her and force warmth—or maybe humanity?—into her.

In that outfit, it was obvious that large sections of her body no longer contained skin. Patches of transparent teal plastic displayed the parts of her body where humanity and technology merged. They could have designed her body to look more normal, at least to the naked eye, but Harrington had wanted it to be obvious she wasn't human. Lucas thought it was pure arrogance.

Thankfully, her face was untouched, and the sections were strategically placed so they could be covered up if needed. Lucas pulled the stopwatch out of his jacket pocket and hit the start button. "Go," he yelled.

She took off like a rocket. She had run this course so many times that she could probably do it in her sleep. He never tired of watching her.

Lucas stared, mesmerized, as she catapulted over the log walls and shimmied down the rope obstacle. His heart caught in his throat when she jumped from one log to the next, and she lost her footing in the rain, spiraling down towards the ground. At the last second, she lunged forward with inhuman agility and grace to grab a rope that swayed in the wind. It should have been a nearly impossible feat, but somehow she managed, and all without breaking a sweat.

She truly was a magnificent creation. Lucas felt his heart swell, partly with pride that he helped build her, but mostly with admiration.

A cold chill ran down his spine, and he was quickly as troubled as the stormy skies as he caught himself thinking of her as a thing he made, rather than a young woman that once was human.

Twenty minutes later, Kaitlyn barreled towards him in a full sprint, her feet sliding in the mud as she came to a stop. He clicked the stop button, and wiped the rain off the screen. A slow smile spread across his face. The recent upgrades had decreased her time by a full two minutes.

"Are you okay?" Lucas asked. "Did you feel anything short out?"

She stared back at him with her vacant, haunted stare. "I'm fine."

"Let's get you back inside so you can get dry. Then you'll need to get a physical to make sure everything is running smoothly."

For a split second, he thought he saw something in her eyes. Some emotion. Boredom maybe? Irritation? He was really losing it. Kaitlyn couldn't feel boredom—or anything else for that matter.

Shivering, he turned back towards the Jeep, trailed by the obedient robot. He opened the passenger door, and she slid into the seat. He wanted to wrap his jacket around her shoulders, but the thought was absurd. Her body was equipped to handle changes in temperature.

They were back at the laboratory within minutes. Once inside, his eyes lingered on her long legs as the nurse wiped them dry. Kaitlyn's hair was plastered to her face, and she still looked gorgeous. Her grey eyes caught his for a second. He wondered what she was thinking, then reminded himself that she wasn't programmed to have idle thoughts.

The computer beeped, saving him from an emotion that felt too much like regret. Lucas pulled his gaze from hers as he turned to the computer and logged onto her server. Everything was running smoothly. The waterproof coating was more than sufficient to protect her delicate robotics. His boss, Harrington, would be pleased.

In only one week, they would be presenting Kaitlyn to government officials. Lucas was still surprised that Dr. Harrington was willing to part with his prized possession. Apparently, notoriety was worth more to him. If the government agreed to take on the project, then Harrington would start on a new and more advanced human. His crazy dream was that someday humans would willingly be subjects, and they would make a super-race. He claimed the only way to do that was to get the government on their side, even if it meant handing over their prototype.

The thought of never seeing Kaitlyn again filled Lucas with despair. Harrington had promised him he would be able to track her project, but inside, Lucas knew better. Once the government was involved, Harrington, Lucas, and the entire unit would be shut out. Their robot girl would disappear into the secretive world of military research and development, and he would never see her again.

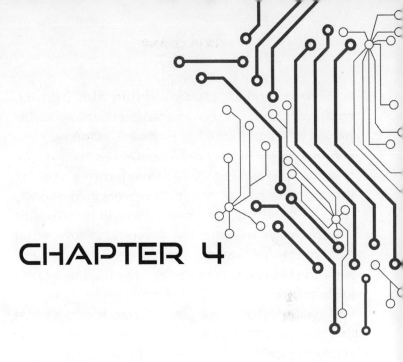

CHAPTER 4

"Quess, what do you know about Lucas?" Kaitlyn twisted a golden maple leaf in her hand as she walked next to her friend in the fading sunlight. Pine needles crunched under foot, like a soft, spongy blanket on the grass muffling their steps.

Quess's face lit up. "Lucas? He's cute, isn't he?"

"Yes, he is physically appealing," Kaitlyn responded, her machinery already whirring to verify her answer. "His face is very symmetrical and pleasing to the eye. However, that's not what I mean. Do you know anything about him as a person?"

Her young friend stooped to pick a taraxacum or the plant commonly known as a dandelion from the ground. "From what I gather, he's some sort of boy genius. He finished his Master's degree when he was seventeen. He's completely dedicated to his work. I don't think he has much of a life outside of IFICS. I know my grandparents have invited him over to dinner, but he always refuses." Quess paused thoughtfully, twirling the brilliant yellow weed between two fingers. "He doesn't seem very social, and I'm pretty sure he's single. Maybe he's just shy."

Well, Kaitlyn thought, at least it wasn't just her that he acted aloof around. Lucas was anti-social in general. That thought was somewhat comforting. Kaitlyn wasn't about to admit she fantasized about Lucas on a regular basis. She couldn't stare at his lips for too long, because she imagined them trailing down her body and spent too long pondering what that might feel like.

No. She definitely couldn't tell Quess that.

"Why do you ask? Do you have a crush on him?" Quess grinned.

"A crush?" Kaitlyn asked, confused. Sometimes she wondered if her and Quess spoke the same language. Kaitlyn was programed to understand and speak seven languages, but she didn't know what her friend was talking about.

"You know... Do you think he's hot?" Quess bit her lip, searching for the words. "Does he rock your world and make butterflies dance in your stomach?"

"I don't know what that means." Kaitlyn tucked a stray strand of her long hair behind her ear. "I just wanted to know more about him. He's so young to be working here with your grandfather."

"I told you, he's a brainiac. Dr. Harrington plucked him from some Ivy League school. I know Gramps is impressed with him. He says 'the young man has a brilliant mind.'" Quess held her hands up, bent down her two first fingers, and said, "Air quote."

The move emphasized the fact that Kaitlyn couldn't understand half of the things Quess said, but she enjoyed the girl's company all the same.

"Did you know that dandelions are edible and in French the name means lion's tooth?"

"Nope, didn't know that." Quess smiled. "It must be strange to have random facts always running through your mind."

Kaitlyn didn't reply. To her it was normal so she didn't know the difference.

It was nice to get outside. Summer was quickly turning into fall. The leaves were beginning to change colors, and the temperature was dropping. Kaitlyn knew they were somewhere in northern Virginia. She had analyzed the dirt and rocks, and compared it to the array of trees. It was mainly the pine trees, dogwoods, and red agate that gave away the location.

Out of curiosity, she had once asked Quess if they *were* in Virginia, and the girl had confirmed it.

Whenever she looked at anything, she analyzed it.

She could look at Quess's floral-print dress and was able to find out it was from American Eagle. Further, she then knew that American Eagle was a popular American store located in almost every mall. She didn't know how she knew this; she just did. The clip in Quess's hair was harder to narrow down because it was sold in so many stores and produced in several countries.

Quess rambled on about her friends and Facebook, which jogged Kaitlyn's memory about their last conversation.

"Did you have any luck with the picture?" Kaitlyn asked nonchalantly, trying to hide her curiosity.

"Not yet. It didn't go quite as easily as I thought. You wouldn't believe how many good looking blond guys there are out there that match your description. I got a lot of hits, but I need to narrow them down. I wish we knew more about your past. You don't recall anything? If we knew where you were from it would help a lot."

"Not really. I just remember the blinding light. And of course, the blond haired guy that always shows up in my dreams. Sometimes I see flashes of scenes, but they don't make any sense." Kaitlyn paused. "You don't think I'm from this area?" She had never given it much thought. It didn't really mater to her where she was from. She couldn't go back.

"No. They wouldn't have taken you from this area. Too many chances of being spotted by someone you know." Quess sounded sure of herself.

That made sense. They put far too much money into the project to risk someone recognizing Kaitlyn. Not that they really needed to worry about that since she was confined to the massive compound. Everything they needed was within the gates which surrounded over one hundred acres. She still had no idea what they planned to do with her. Everyone kept saying she was almost ready. Ready for what?

"You don't have an accent, so it's hard to say. Do you think they changed the way you talk?"

"I wouldn't be surprised." Kaitlyn had no idea how much they had altered her. Sometimes she wondered what she used to like to do. She must have had hobbies, a favorite food, a family....

"I'll poke around and see if I can find anything out," Quess went on. "Maybe Nanny will spill some secrets. She's always been a bit of a gossip."

Kaitlyn stopped and pivoted on her toes to look at the girl. "Do you think she knows anything about who I was?"

Quess flipped her copper braid over her shoulder. "Who knows? But if anyone does, I would say it was her. My grandparents have been married nearly fifty years. I think they tell each other everything."

Kaitlyn found that hard to believe, but didn't want to dissuade Quess. She seemed to enjoy the mystery, and it gave her something to do. The girl had said many times how boring it was spending the summer with her grandparents. At least Quess was able to leave the compound to go shopping with her grandmother. That seemed to make her happy. Kaitlyn secretly wished she was able to join them on their outings, if for no other reason then to see if the human world reminded her of who she had been.

"Why don't you come over for dinner sometime?" Quess asked, her eyes lit with excitement.

"You know I don't have to eat." Kaitlyn continued down the path, watching leaves float to the ground as they fell from the trees.

"But you can, right? If you wanted to?"

"Yes, I can eat enough to pass me off as *human* if needed." The words made her flinch. The computer side of her thought of humans as inferior, for they lacked the brain she possessed.

The human side of her, however, longed to know more.

"Then it's settled. Tomorrow, you will come over for dinner, and we can grill Nanny on your past," Quess said.

A part of Kaitlyn was curious to find out more about her past, but another part didn't want to know. What good would it do to find out she had family and friends who thought she was dead? It wasn't like she could just stroll back into her old life and start over. No, that life was dead and buried. It should stay that way.

I think.

"Does your grandmother know about our talks?" she asked.

"Kaitlyn, I can't believe you would ask that. We pinky promised, remember?"

Kaitlyn smiled at the memory. For some reason, a pinky promise was very important to Quess. Kaitlyn had thought it was very strange at the time, but a feeling of warmth had come over her after the exchange.

"I remember."

"How am I going to be a spy if I can't even keep a simple promise? You can trust me, Kaitlyn. I know I'm just a kid, but my word means something."

"I like you, Quess. You are the only person to treat me like more than a robot. If it weren't for your warning to keep my memories to myself, who knows what else they would have done to me. For that you have my loyalty."

Quess smiled. "And you have mine. I'm sorry they did this to you, but I'm glad they saved your life. This summer would have really sucked without you around."

They continued their walk around the compound. After the sun faded completely, they said their goodbyes, and Kaitlyn returned to the white walls of her room.

Aware of how alone she was without Quess, Kaitlyn settled into bed for another dream-filled night.

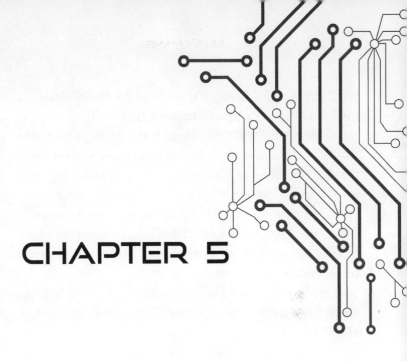

CHAPTER 5

Lucas would rather be going anywhere else tonight, but he hadn't been able to say no. Professor Adams insisted, and when that man got something in his head there was no changing it. He was like a bulldog with a bone.

Lucas held up two shirts: A light blue oxford and a white oxford. He eyed them warily, lifting first one then the other up to the light. He wished he had someone to help him make these decisions. His cat domino rubbed against his leg. "What do you think domino? Blue or white?" The cat purred.

"A lot of help you are."

He could compute equations in his mind, but couldn't decide what to wear. Ridiculous.

Picking out a shirt shouldn't be this difficult, he told himself. Hanging the white shirt back on the rack, he shrugged into the blue. He always wore white to work. It was the logical decision. Maybe he should expand his wardrobe, but since signing on with IFICS his social life had taken a back seat.

Fumbling with the buttons, Lucas wondered what was so important that Adams couldn't talk to him tomorrow at work. Didn't they see enough of each other as it was.

He hoped there weren't more big changes in store for Kaitlyn. Every time they did an upgrade, she became less and less human. They were robbing her of her life experiences—memories of old ones and the pleasure in new ones. They were piece by piece removing her soul. Soon, all she would have left was the technology and not the person. If there was even anything left. After the first operation, she still smiled at him, still let out a half-amused breath when he tripped over the power cords. After the second upgrade, she stopped laughing. By the fifth, she stopped smiling entirely. Guilt washed over Lucas, and as hard as he tried to push it away, a permanent, low level of uneasiness stayed with him.

It was an hour's drive to the compound, which was ridiculous since it hadn't even been an hour and a half since he'd left work. And here he was, headed back in the same direction. On the bright side, IFICS reimbursed him for mileage and gas.

IFICS did a lot for Lucas. The job really was a dream-come-true. Great pay, generous benefits, and work he loved. Seriously, what more could he ask for?

If only his conscience hadn't started to bother him. Without knowing why he was doing it, Lucas had started planning escape routes for Kaitlyn. He shook his head at the thought, gripping the steering wheel tighter turning his knuckles white. He must be losing his mind.

Every time he saw her, he wanted to whisk her away from the life she was headed towards. Hell, the life she was living. Who was he kidding. Guilt wrenched his body knowing he was practically the mastermind behind morphing her into a cyborg. If it weren't for his coding, they wouldn't have been able to get as far as they had.

He felt repulsed by himself — for what he had done, and for the fact that he was so drawn to her in her half human form.

It didn't help that she was gorgeous: those long legs, dark hair, athletic body, and incredible mind. It was the last one that made his heart trip up. God, she was so intelligent. The amount of information stored in her beautiful brain was mind-boggling. It was like she was a living, walking encyclopedia. In his eyes she was perfection, at least until they kept stripping away who she had been little by little. Now she was an empty shell of what she had been.

Lucas shook his head — he had issues.

He drove the rest of the way lost in his thoughts. Before he knew it, he saw the sign — Private Property. Trespassers Will Be Shot. The sign was not a joke. Lucas looked up and saw the silhouette of an armed guard patrolling the grounds. Well-trained guards stood on alert throughout the property, most of them ex-Special Forces and armed with the kind of weaponry that was probably illegal in seven countries. It was a constant reminder of the importance of the project.

Dr. Harrington spared no expense. As a billionaire, he could pretty much do whatever the hell he wanted, which was how IFICS was formed. It wasn't even an acronym, IFICS didn't even mean anything. Harrington's dry sense of humor had thought it would be funny to name his company IFICS: Sci-fi backwards. Lucas smiled to himself. It was clever — he had to give him that.

Harrington had always been obsessed with the future and advances in technology, not to mention his own desire to live forever. His company was on the cutting edge of science as far as anti-aging, and he had made tremendous gains in the field. The company was known for nanobots used to dramatically slow the process of aging. Harrington was sixty-three and barely looked forty. Modern miracle.

But Kaitlyn was the real dream. The secret project. Now that Kaitlyn was turning out to be a success, Harrington had started to get greedy. The eccentric man had begun to believe that cyborgs—like Kaitlyn—were the way of the future. In fifty years, he believed it would be normal, she would be normal, and so would thousands of other cyborgs living out their lives among the human populace. Lucas didn't quite believe that, but he kept his thoughts to himself.

He hadn't seen the man in quite some time. Professor Adams had informed him Harrington was off in the rainforest hunting exotic wild animals or something equally as crazy. The man had a death wish, but fate always seemed to shine on his side. Some people were just lucky that way. A man with a death wish that wanted to live forever. Makes total sense, Lucas thought wryly.

Of course, Harrington would have to return soon before the government bid on Kaitlyn. Lucas knew there was no chance he would miss that. His vision becoming a reality.

He rolled his Jeep to a stop at the guard gate and nodded to Sam who had a high powered rifle slung over his shoulder.

"What are you doing back?"

"I know, right?" Lucas said, "Adams called me back in. I'd just got home."

Lucas handed his pass to the burly guard. The older man's arms were as big as Lucas's neck.

Sam grunted and handed Lucas his ID. Lucas nodded in thanks and put his Jeep in drive and crept through the gated entry. Night had already fallen and a full moon hung high in the sky. Giving the compound an eerie glow.

Who would have thought that at only twenty he would have such a highly classified job? Certainly not his father, not that he had stayed around to see how Lucas turned out.

Pushing the negative thoughts aside, Lucas drove towards the back of the compound. He pulled into a parking spot and jumped out. Professor Adams's stone cottage stood off in the distance with a wisp of smoke billowing from the chimney, looking for all the world like an idyllic cottage in the countryside. Very out of place, but Harrington wanted Adams to live on the compound in case any issues arose. The cottage had been Mrs. Adams idea. She said if she was going to be stuck on the god forsaken compound she might as well get her dream house. Harrington had built it to her specifics. Harrington definitely took care of his own. He had to give him that.

Lucas trudged forward across the well-manicured lawn and rang the doorbell. He just wanted the night to be over with.

Mrs. Adams opened the door with a friendly smile, her white hair falling in loose curls around her face. It was obvious the woman had been a looker in her day, but time had taken a toll, and had deeply lined her oval face and high cheekbones. Her bright blue eyes, however, still sparkled with youthfulness.

The Adams's didn't believe in the anti-aging treatments that IFICS had invented, but they were okay with turning a girl into half a human. People rarely made sense.

"Come in, Lucas. So glad you could join us." She stepped aside and allowed him to pass into the cottage. He could smell fresh baked bread cooking. The aroma was mouth watering.

"You look as lovely as ever, Mrs. Adams."

"Oh, you. Keep 'em coming. You know I'm a sucker for compliments," she gave him an impish grin that took years off her face.

A stone fireplace sat to the right, lit with flames. Knickknacks covered the worn wooden shelves that lined both sides. From the look of the shelves, the mantle, and end tables, Mrs. Adams collected angels and porcelain bears. A worn leather couch and two rocking chairs filled the small room. He smiled at the sight of the brightly colored rug in front of the fireplace. It reminded him of a rug his mother had made by hand many years ago. His mothers didn't turn out quite as nice, but at least she tried. His mom always tried.

"Dinner is almost ready," Mrs. Adams said sweetly. "I made roast. I hope that's okay with you. You're not vegetarian, are you? If so, I can whip something up."

"Roast is fine. Thank you, it smells amazing." He'd had no idea he was coming for dinner; he had thought it was just a last minute meeting with the Professor. The sound of his stomach rumbling reminded him he hadn't eaten since lunch, so a home cooked dinner was a welcome surprise.

"Take off your jacket and join the rest of us in the sitting room."

Lucas shrugged out of his jacket and wondered who 'the rest of us' were. He hoped he wasn't being ambushed with some crazy upgrade by the professor. They were too close to make drastic changes now.

Mrs. Adams took his jacket and walked away to hang it in a nearby closet.

"Follow me." She smiled and led him down a narrow hallway lined with black and white photographs.

He almost stumbled over his own feet when he saw Kaitlyn sitting on a floral loveseat next to the Adams's granddaughter.

What is Kaitlyn doing here?

Kaitlyn looked up and caught his gaze. He felt like a lovesick teenager. His heart raced, and his mouth felt dry and refused to cooperate; he needed to say something, but nothing would come out. She literally took his breath away.

She sat at the edge of the loveseat holding a

glass of water. The white dress she was wearing was entirely too revealing. Her long legs were pressed together and tilted to the side. He could see the coding scroll through her calves, and he had to force himself to look away. He searched the room until his eyes settled on a painting in the corner. It was black, red, and white and he had no idea what it was supposed to depict. It looked like a bunch of paint splatters to him, but something told him it was worth a fortune.

"Lucas, I'm so glad you could join us tonight," Professor Adams said, offering a hand. "My wife has been dying to have you as a dinner guest for some time."

"A dinner guest?" Lucas sputtered, shaking his superior's hand. "I thought you had to see me about work?"

The elder man tutted. "My dear boy. Sometimes work needs to be set aside, and we just need to enjoy one another's company."

Lucas felt like he was being set up, but he had no idea why. What could that Adam's possible want with him.

CHAPTER 6

What is he doing here? Tearing her eyes away from Lucas she glanced at Quess.

Kaitlyn stared blankly at the girl, but Quess just smiled innocently back. Kaitlyn had a feeling Quess knew all along. She really was good at keeping secrets.

She should have told her that Lucas was coming for dinner. Not that it would have made a difference. She was interested in seeing him outside of the clinical environment.

Taking a deep breath, Kaitlyn composed herself. She could do this. It was just dinner after all, and Lucas had no idea of her hidden desire to rip his clothes off and trail her lips up the length of his body. She felt heat rush to her face, but her system quickly regulated it.

He looked even more attractive than usual tonight. The light blue button-up matched his eyes, making them stand out even more, and it was unbuttoned at the top, revealing a white t-shirt underneath. His khaki pants hung loosely at his hips and stretched over his muscular thighs. Kaitlyn absently wondered when he had time to work out. He seemed to always be at the lab.

Lucas shifted from one foot to the other. A sign that he was uncomfortable. He seemed just as shocked to see her as she was to see him. He shoved his hands in his pockets and then pulled them out as if he was unsure what to do with his hands.

His gaze settled on her as he said, "Kaitlyn, it's nice to see you here. I didn't know you visited the Adams's home."

His rich, deep voice sent a strange feeling down her spine. It was almost as if a chill were in the air even though the fireplace ensured the room was a warm seventy-eight degrees, according to Kaitlyn's internal thermometer.

The sensations Lucas caused within her were confusing, and she was unable to process the meaning. When she scanned her mind, it came up blank. *Yet again proof that computers don't know everything*, she thought, slightly annoyed.

"This is the first time I have been," Kaitlyn said. "Quess invited me for dinner."

At least her mind and mouth were cooperating; that wasn't always the case in the presence of Lucas. Her hands were clammy with sweat, and her stomach felt funny. She wondered if that was what Quess meant by butterflies dancing in her stomach.

"Nanny, it smells like dinner is ready," Quess interjected, saving Kaitlyn from the awkwardness.

Mrs. Adams sniffed the air, and then leveled her gaze on her granddaughter. "Why, yes, I do believe you're right, dear. Let's all go to the kitchen."

Kaitlyn rose swiftly, turning on her heel and heading in the direction of the kitchen with the rest of them close behind. The smell of roast beef, fresh bread and potatoes triggered something in Kaitlyn, but it was like a scratch she couldn't itch. The feeling caused a tingling in her memory; so close, but not close enough. To say it was annoying would be an understatement. This sometimes happened with certain scents. She wasn't sure what it meant and wished she could ask Lucas or Professor Adams, but that would be giving away too much.

The kitchen was rustic and well-used. There was very little wall space that wasn't covered in pale wood cabinets, and the thin area of space above was hung with old cast iron skillets and copper pots. It was five degrees warmer in the space than the rest of the house.

"Have a seat anywhere," Mrs. Adams declared, waving her hands towards the large oval dining room table that sat in an alcove next to the kitchen. The table was covered with bright yellow placemats, and floral napkins.

Hesitating, Kaitlyn waited until the others were seated so she wouldn't take the wrong chair. Mr. Adams sat at the head of the table, as she expected, Lucas sat to the right of him, and Quess sat at the other end next to what would presumably be her grandmother's seat.

Kaitlyn made her way around the table and sat across from Quess, unfolding her napkin and placing it in her lap. Like she saw Quess do. There was one seat separating her from Lucas.

He tugged at his t-shirt collar as if it were choking him. His cheeks were flushed. She wondered if it was from the heat of the fireplace.

What is he thinking? Kaitlyn wondered. What was it that made him so uncomfortable? Quess had said he was anti-social. Maybe he was uncomfortable eating around others, but that seemed odd even to her.

Lucas cleared his throat. "Professor Adams, I don't mean to sound ungrateful, but what is the meaning of this meeting?"

Professor Adams gave a half-smile, helping himself to the pitcher of iced tea in the center of the table. "Beats the hell out of me. Ask the women of this family. I'm just as surprised as you are." He filled his glass and then filled his wives. "The sooner you learn women rule this world, the better off you'll be."

Just then Mrs. Adams walked in, carrying a large plate of roast beef, the thinly sliced meat pink at the center. Her smile lit up the room. "Ain't that the truth!"

She set the platter on the table and retreated back to the kitchen. Quess rose and hurried to help her grandmother. Soon, the table was filled with roast, potatoes, rolls, and vegetables.

The scents were wonderful, but Kaitlyn dreaded having to eat. The roast would taste no different to her than the potatoes. It was as if her taste buds had been removed, but more than likely it was a computer chip that overrode those senses. Sometimes she wished she could tear out all the sensors.

But then again, what would that leave of Kaitlyn? Would she even be able to survive without the mechanics? She really had no idea.

Quess tapped Kaitlyn on the arm. "Help yourself."

It seemed they all watched as Kaitlyn placed a small portion of roast, potatoes, and green beans on her plate. She bypassed the rolls. That would have been too much for her to eat. Her internal encyclopedia informed her of protocols of etiquette and leaving food on one's plate would be offensive to the host. She didn't want to offend Mrs. Adams.

Quess reached across Kaitlyn to grab a golden roll. "Hey, Gramps, I was thinking that you should add a slang chip to Kaitlyn. Half the time she has no idea what I'm talking about."

Kaitlyn's eyes snapped in the direction of Professor Adams. He rubbed his chin, lost in thought. "You know that's actually a great idea, Quess."

Quess smiled, obviously proud of herself.

"What do you think, Lucas?" Professor Adams stared at Lucas, awaiting his response.

Lucas shrugged. "I don't think it could hurt. If they want her to mix with the general population, it makes sense she would need to understand colloquialisms. I can work on a program tomorrow."

Professor Adams nodded. "Very good. Thank you, Quess. I would have never thought of such a thing on my own."

Kaitlyn watched the exchange, only somewhat interested. It was as if they were talking about a stranger and not herself. She didn't really care if she could understand slang, as they called it. It wasn't as if she had a say in the matter anyway. They always did what they wanted without consulting her.

At least the idea seemed to make Quess happy. The girl's round cheeks were flushed, and her eyes shone with pride at her grandfather's compliments.

Then Kaitlyn's sensors alerted her to something she'd missed during the conversation. Lucas had said *the general population*. Kaitlyn took that to mean she was going to leave the compound. The thought was equally as exciting as it was terrifying.

"Professor Adams, I am curious. Where did I live before moving here?" Kaitlyn asked between bites of roast.

She was met with silence. Kaitlyn wasn't sure if it was the question itself, or that no one had expected her to speak.

She watched as a look passed between Lucas and the professor.

"Why do you ask?" Professor Adams asked calmly, setting his fork on the table and wiping his mouth on his napkin.

"I was just wondering. Virginia does not feel like home." Kaitlyn took a sip of water and waited for their reply.

All eyes, even Quess's, were wide and shocked. Kaitlyn realized she had made a mistake.

"Feel, Kaitlyn?" the professor asked. "Please, explain what you mean by 'not feeling like home.'" Professor Adams focused his attention solely on Kaitlyn.

Her machinery kicked in, and her coded neurons warned her processing center that the situation was an uneasy one. One moment of analysis and she realized why — she had used the word 'felt.'

She meant it. Something inside her recalled some *place*, and she couldn't figure out how or why or where. It bothered her when she couldn't understand things. She was supposed to be a superior being, and yet the littlest things made no sense to her.

But the professor — and Lucas — couldn't know that.

She considered her words carefully. "I don't know. Quess was telling me she grew up in Ohio. I must be from somewhere else. I have no idea where I grew up."

The professor's shoulders seemed to relax. "Perhaps because where you were from did not experience the drastic season changes. Summer is turning into fall, is that what you mean?"

Kaitlyn thought about his answer for a moment before replying. Her computer banks immediately began to filter through states and weather patterns. The professor had narrowed down where she was from without realizing it. "Perhaps, the change of season is what is triggering the random thought. It doesn't matter where I am from. What matters is I am here now."

The professor smiled, satisfied. Lucas, however, looked paler than usual.

They could use this information to narrow

down the blond haired guy, and perhaps learn something about her past.

Blacksburg Branch

Phone: 540 552 8246

§

Date 6/3/2015 Time: 11:27:57 AM

Name: Shamim, Faatimah

Fines/Fees Owed: $0.00

Items checked out this session: 3

Title: Legacy
Barcode: 50722013865520
Due Date: 6/24/2015,23:59 (*)

Title: The gatekeeper's sons
Barcode: 50722014085557
Due Date: 6/24/2015,23:59

Title: Freak of nature
Barcode: 50722014077885
Due Date: 6/24/2015,23:59

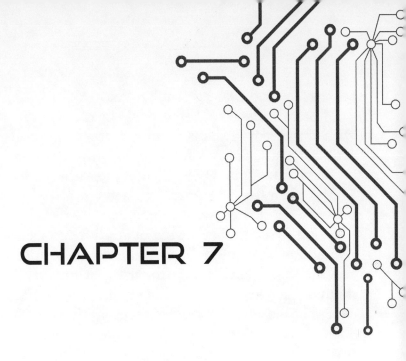

CHAPTER 7

Professor Adams attached the blood pressure cuff to Kaitlyn's arm and turned away, one fist pumping the small bag and filling the cuff with air. "Don't move," he told her, his eyes on the gauge.

This would be a good time to roll her eyes Kaitlyn thought. As if she would have moved.

While her arm was slowly gripped tighter and tighter by the cuff, Kaitlyn sensed someone coming down the hall, but they were too far away to determine who it was. Hopefully, it was Lucas—she hadn't seen him all day. He was probably working on the new coding, the 'slang' they had spoken of at dinner. The day seemed longer when he was not around. She longed to see his face and hear his familiar voice.

Instead, she had been stuck inside all day with Professor Adams running tests on her artificial heart. Thirty minutes at maximum speed on the treadmill, and then a blood pressure check. Thirty minutes of sitting still, then a blood pressure check. Boring. Monotonous.

Kaitlyn glanced at the old man. His spectacles had slid so far down his nose it was a surprise they hadn't fallen off. Not for the first time, she thought she should have hated him for taking away her old life, but for some reason, she didn't. She only felt indifference for the professor and the rest of the staff. They had probably programmed her that way.

Kaitlyn was tired of never knowing which thoughts were her own, and which were IFICS.

"Well done." The professor pulled apart the velcro and released Kaitlyn from the cuff.

Like I have anything to do with my blood pressure. I don't even have a normal heart. With all her knowledge she couldn't even comprehend how her body was able to function properly. A medical marvel was often thrown around in regards to her body.

The professor rolled his chair around where Kaitlyn was sitting to glance at the computer screen. It was hooked up to electrodes placed on her chest. Adams was obsessed with bio-rhythmics, and was constantly tracking all her numbers searching for any anomalies. He said it was the mathematician in him. Bio-rhythmics consisted of three cycles: physical, emotional and intellectual. It didn't seem very scientific to her.

"Amazing." He muttered staring at the data. "Your readings are always the same. No matter what we do to you."

There was a knock at the door, and Frank, her firearms instructor, entered the room. "Time for the shooting range."

Finally, something that wasn't boring. Kaitlyn had to suppress a smile that wanted to spread across her face. After her initial training, she only spent one day a week on the range. Frank claimed she was so accurate, anymore time would just be a waste of bullets. They just wanted to keep her from getting rusty.

She was quite sure her parts could not rust, but she kept her thoughts to herself.

With haste she made her way to the arms room and grabbed her gear.

There was something calming about the feel of cold steel in her hand. It was as if the gun was an extension of her hand.

Maybe they were right. Maybe she *was* born for this. Or maybe she would never know since she couldn't recall her life before the accident.

Kaitlyn slammed a fresh magazine into the Browning MK III. Legs planted firmly, she leaned forward just a little, arms locked, and lined up the red dot. Letting out a breath, she squeezed the trigger repeatedly in rapid succession.

She lowered the pistol and pushed the button to the right of her. The electronic carrier brought the black silhouette forward, edges of the paper waving in the breeze as it moved.

Her instructor, Frank, whistled under his breath and stared at the quarter-sized hole in the middle of the target's bulbous forehead. "Damn girl. Forty-five meters. That's the stuff of legends."

"Legends?" Kaitlyn asked, staring at Frank. He was a big guy—broad shoulders, a huge, muscular torso, and a neck as thick as a tree trunk. Kaitlyn had to peer up at him he was so tall.

Frank stared at her, but didn't reply. He ran his hand through his greying goatee and he opened his mouth about to say something, but thought better of it and clamped his mouth. He wasn't allowed to talk to her unless it was in regards to training. He turned his back on her and jerked down the target. "Let's try that again. Only this time, left arm only."

Kaitlyn waited patiently as Frank attached two new targets and hit the switch to send them back down the training field. He stepped away and motioned. "Two to the chest, one to the head."

She nodded and got in position. Frank moved

the targets this time, back and forth and side to side. She calculated the distance and squeezed the trigger. As the targets continued to move, Kaitlyn's mind kept up with them as if they were standing still. Moving targets were so much more fun than stationary.

"Come over here and let's work a few different drills." Frank walked away, not bothering to check if she was following. Shaking his head, he shot back over his shoulder, "Before long you will be teaching me drills I've never heard of."

Kaitlyn slid the pistol into its holster and followed behind her firearms instructor to the shooting box.

Across the field was a set of six steel plates in the shape of human heads, each about 8 inches in diameter and arranged side by side on a supporting stand.

"Okay, load and make ready."

Automatically, Kaitlyn removed her pistol from its holster and locked the slide to the rear. She quickly checked the chamber to ensure it was empty, then removed a full magazine from her magazine carrier on her left hip and inserted the magazine into the pistol, the motion so smooth and practiced it felt natural. With a flick of her thumb, the slide slammed forward, loading a round into the chamber of the pistol. She then conducted a 'press check,' reaching underneath the pistol, pinching the slide, and moving it to the rear just enough to see that a round was actually in the chamber. Seeing the brass, she released the slide and holstered her weapon.

Standing in the shooter's box, she faced the steel plates, hands at her sides and waited. Without turning, she knew Lucas was near. Sometimes he came to observe her during target practice. He never mentioned it, but she always knew when he was near. She liked knowing he was close by.

The instructor moved to her right rear, reset his shot timer and said,

"Shooter ready?"

Kaitlyn nodded her head once, affirming that she was ready.

"Stand by…" and then there was a loud "BEEP" from the timer.

Kaitlyn immediately drew her pistol and punched it straight out, arms extended in what was known as position four. She already had the sights lined up and on the left-most target before her arms were even straight. As she reached full extension, she pressed the trigger and then moved the pistol to the second target, using both the momentum of the pistol's recoil and her own muscle movement. As soon as the sights were on the second target, she fired again, repeating the process a total of six times with a metallic "ping" punctuating every gunshot.

Once she was done, Frank barked, "Unload and show clear."

Kaitlyn complied, movements quick. Reflexive.

"Holster."

She shoved the gun into position and let her hands dangle at her sides expectantly. In the back of her mind wondered what Lucas was doing. She could sense he was approximately fifty yards behind her to the left. It gave her a slight thrill knowing he was watching her when she was in her element.

Looking down at the timer, the instructor raised an eyebrow and said, "Two-point-three-five seconds. Lets do that again, this time from right to left." He reset the targets, and then went through the same series of instructions for her to 'Load and make ready' and 'Standby.' The timer went off, and Kaitlyn repeated her performance.

"Two-point-three-seven." Frank eyed her as if he wanted to say something else, but shook his head instead. "Alright then, let's move over to the next apparatus."

They walked to another shooting box in front of three steel targets that were twelve inches square, three meters apart from each other, and ten meters down range. Kaitlyn stole a glance back at Lucas. He lifted his hand and waved. She felt her fake heart flutter.

"This drill is called 'El Presidente.' I want you

to have two magazines of six rounds each. Face 'up range,' back to targets, hands at your sides. On the buzzer, you'll turn, draw, and engage each target with two rounds before indexing to the next target. Upon slide lock, conduct a magazine change, then re-engage targets in the opposite direction, again with two rounds each. Any questions?"

Having none, Kaitlyn didn't say anything as she started setting up her magazines per instructions. Once that was done, the instructor went through the range commands again, and then the buzzer sounded.

BAM, BAM, BAM, BAM, BAM, BAM... click click, BAM, BAM, BAM, BAM, BAM, BAM.

"Unload and show clear. Holster. Three-point-nine-five seconds. That's..." he paused to self-censor himself, "... unheard of. Let's try that strong-hand only."

She continued to shoot the various drills the instructor set-up and explained. Each time, unknown to Kaitlyn, she performed at a world class level, something that took competition shooters years of practice and hundreds of thousands of rounds. She did it all without question, without hesitation, and with near-perfect precision.

As they finished, the instructor said. "Maybe I can get the docs to wire me up...." He grinned and shook his head.

Kaitlyn stared at him expressionless.

"Okay, we're done here." Frank took off his ear protection. "Clean your piece and put it in the safe."

She nodded and broke down the gun. She turned to the left and watched as Lucas walked back towards the lab without a word to her—as usual.

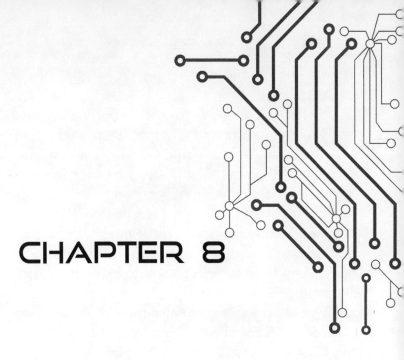

CHAPTER 8

The next day the door to the lab opened, and Quess peeked around the corner. Kaitlyn had never seen Quess in the lab. "Gramps, can Kaitlyn come out with me? Please?"

Professor Adams glanced at the clock on the wall. "You know you're not supposed to come in here, Quess."

Professor Adams had strict rules about who could be in the lab and for what reasons. Kaitlyn knew whatever had brought her young friend there must have been important.

Quess shrugged and entered the room. "I'm bored, and it's your lunch time, anyway. I already ate with Nanny. She wanted me to bring you the leftovers." She handed him a plate that was covered in foil.

"Fine, we're done for now. But make sure she's back in an hour." The professor's wrinkled face softened into a smile. Anyone else would have been thrown out for stepping foot into his sacred space without asking, but his granddaughter had always been an exception.

The professor peeled off the bio-rhythmic cuff and released Kaitlyn's arm from the monitor. She stood, happy to have a reason to leave the stuffy room.

Quess pulled her sweater tight over her chest and looked Kaitlyn over. "It's cold outside."

"It's sixty-one degrees," Kaitlyn said matter-of-factly.

Quess eyed at Kaitlyn's long, bare legs. "You should put on some clothes."

"I have on clothes."

Quess sighed. "Fine. Don't blame me if you get a cold."

Professor Adams laughed and chucked her chin. "Quess, she can't get a cold. You know that."

"How could I forget? You made her non-human," Quess snapped.

"I've heard enough from you, young lady." The professor's playful tone evaporated and his voice brokered no argument. "We've been over this many times before. Now you hurry along before I change my mind."

Kaitlyn watched the exchange with interest. She found it curious that Quess would argue with her grandfather over her.

Without another word, Quess turned on her heels in a huff and stalked from the room. Kaitlyn trailed after her.

Quess banged through the metal doors and into the bright sunshine outside, where they walked in silence until they were at a safe distance from the building and cameras. Kaitlyn watched as the wind gently stirred the leaves around them.

"You wasted a perfectly good opportunity, you know," Quess finally spoke up, clearly irritated. "I can't believe you didn't grill them more at dinner. We could have found out something about your past."

A cursory scan told Kaitlyn that Quess's little round face was pinched and annoyed. The girl's heart rate was also elevated, showing signs of distress.

Kaitlyn smiled. "We gained significant information. How many states do not show signs of season changes?"

Quess stopped in her tracks and turned slowly, her frown turning into a grin. "How many?"

Pulling up the file she had saved to her memory drive the evening before, Kaitlyn said, "Florida, Nevada, Arizona, California and

Louisiana are a starting point. Should that help in your search?"

"Definitely. I wish you could come home with me to the cottage." Quess sighed. "It would be much easier if we could get on my computer together."

"I don't think that is going to happen. I'm surprised they let you spend as much time as they do with me."

"Gramps would prefer I don't see you at all, but Nanny convinced him I need some sort of friend around here, even if it is with a robot." Quess smiled wryly.

"Thank your Nanny for me."

"I can't do that. That would give away our secret."

Kaitlyn smiled; she really did enjoy the girl's company. Quess seemed to have that effect on everyone around her. She made it hard for Kaitlyn to keep her all-too-human feelings hidden. She didn't try very hard around Quess. Being with her she was able to let her guard down. At least briefly.

"So, I think Lucas is totally digging you."

"Digging me?" Kaitlyn tried to make sense of the phrase. Maybe she really did need a slang chip. She could not think of any way that 'dig' would have anything to do with her. Dig: 1. to break up, turn over, or remove earth, sand, etc., as with a shovel, spade, bulldozer, or claw; make an excavation. 2. to make one's way or work by or as by removing or turning over material: *to dig through the files*. None of those definitions matched the context.

"Yeah, did you see his face when he walked in and saw you last night? He totally wants you."

Kaitlyn had no idea how to respond. "I don't understand what you are saying."

"It means he likes you. He totally has the hots for you."

Kaitlyn's body felt hyper aware, her senses tingling. "You really think so?" Perhaps, Lucas thought of tearing off her clothes like she did his. Somehow she highly doubt it though. The odd were not in her favor. After all she wasn't even really human anymore.

"Definitely, it was written all over his face. Thankfully, Gramps is oblivious, but even Nanny noticed he's crushing on you. She thinks you two would make a cute couple."

Kaitlyn hadn't noticed anything on his face. Perhaps Quess was imagining things. She did seem to have an overactive imagination—one of the reasons Kaitlyn enjoyed the girl's company so much. It was nice to see things through her human eyes.

"Aren't you at least a little excited?"

"About what?" Kaitlyn asked confused.

"Lucas! He likes you. You're obviously interested in him or you wouldn't have asked."

"Oh. I don't really know what to think about that."

Quess sighed. "I wish you felt things like a normal person."

"Me, too." Kaitlyn said softly.

"So what are you going to do if we find the mystery man?" Quess asked curiously.

Kaitlyn hadn't thought that far ahead. But really, what could she do? Show up on his door step and say *Remember me?* That probably wouldn't go over well. "Maybe we should stop the search."

"What? Are you kidding me? No way. I need something to keep me busy at night. I'm going to find him, plus it will help sharpen my secret spy skills. You know...just in case."

"I guess that's true," Kaitlyn agreed.

After they made their loop around the grounds, Kaitlyn sighed. "We need to get back to the lab. Professor Adams says this new update is important."

"I don't know how you put up with them always changing you." Quess turned and they headed back towards the laboratory.

"It's annoying, but I know that's what I'm here for."

"I wish they would just leave you alone. It's not fair." Tears welled up in Quess's eyes, making them look more green than hazel.

Kaitlyn felt a lump form in her throat, but she

wasn't sure why. "It's okay, Quess. I don't mind."

"But you should." She balled her small fists up by her sides. Her pale face was bright pink, and a teardrop escaped, trailing down her cheek. "You should have a normal life. Not caged away like some animal. You can't even comprehend how wrong this is, that's the worst part."

Kaitlyn watched the young girl swipe tears away, and wondered what it felt like to cry. She hoped it wasn't painful for her friend.

"Does this hurt?" Kaitlyn touched the liquid seeping down Quess's cheek.

Quess giggled. "Crying?"

Kaitlyn inclined her head. "Yes."

"No. Crying doesn't hurt." Quess sobered, using the sleeve of her cardigan to wipe away her tears. She reached for Kaitlyn's hand and took hold, bringing her hand to her chest. Reflexively Kaitlyn tried to pull her hand from Quess grasp. But Quess just held on tighter. Kaitlyn's hand relaxed.

Beneath Kaitlyn's palm, she felt the sensation of Quess's human heart beating slowly and consistently.

Quess held tightly to Kaitlyn's hand, keeping it spread over her heart. "Crying doesn't hurt. But when you cry, it's because your heart does."

"Your heart hurts for me?" Kaitlyn asked, puzzled. Though Quess's strong grip was a little unsettling to her sensors, there was something deep inside her that reveled in the way her friend's heart beat steadily; reveled in her warmth and kindness. That lump in her throat wouldn't go away.

Quess just nodded as more tears filled her eyes.

"Let's get back inside," Kaitlyn said, still trying to process the information. She pulled away from Quess. "Maybe they are upgrading my slang vocabulary, and our conversations won't be so perplexing."

Quess broke into a laugh, a wonderful sound to Kaitlyn's ears, but she stopped laughing as quickly as she started. "Are they really making you leave next week?"

"What? Where did you hear that?"

"I overheard my grandparents talking. They said that you were almost complete, and it was nearly time to hand you over to fulfill your destiny."

"My destiny?" Kaitlyn felt like she couldn't breathe. That was ridiculous; there was nothing blocking her airways.

As much as she disliked the compound, she didn't want to leave. Where were they going to send her? She ran scenarios through her mind and came up empty. She had no idea. Her infinite source of knowledge couldn't give her an answer.

And that was terrifying.

As much as she hated to admit it, she had come

to enjoy her time with Professor Adams and his bushy eyebrows, Lucas well because he's Lucas; even the nurse who never spoke a word to her. The daily routine with them made her feel *almost* normal.

She didn't want to think about never seeing Quess or Lucas again. She couldn't. Her mind rebelled at the thought. "There must be some kind of mistake."

Quess didn't bother to reply.

Kaitlyn pushed through the double doors. Lucas was sitting behind the desk in the large laboratory and stood up immediately when she walked through. He hit a stack of file folders with his hip, and the tower slid to the floor, papers exploding out. A vial crashed to the ground and splintered off into hundreds of shards.

"Well, that was graceful." Lucas picked up a file from the floor.

"Is it true?" Kaitlyn demanded.

"Is what true?" Lucas asked, tearing his gaze away from the mess to her, his mouth slightly agape.

"Am I leaving the compound to go on assignment?"

Lucas looked away and wouldn't meet her eye and instead, knelt and stuffed pages back into files.

Confirmation. Quess told her never to trust

someone that won't look you in the eyes. She felt like she was running, but she was standing still. Her body was revved up, even though she was rooted to the floor.

"Does it bother you? The thought of leaving?" Lucas asked, finally catching her gaze.

"It doesn't matter to me." Kaitlyn kept her voice level. "Will I return?"

Lucas's expression changed and mirrored the look that had been on Quess's face earlier before she had started crying. *His heart hurts.* In that moment, she knew she would never set foot on the compound again. Never see Lucas again. She wondered if they were going to send her on a suicide mission in order to shut down the project. She saw a movie about that once. Or maybe they would just hand her off to new owners. Kaitlyn didn't know which idea sounded worse.

"We need to upgrade your hardware. I want to add facial expressions to your database that you can filter through to make conversations easier. It will help you react to situations if you know what emotion the person is feeling. You will eventually learn to mimic expressions as well."

"Fine." Kaitlyn resigned to accept whatever was coming her way. Of course, he wouldn't tell her anything.

"Please take a seat." Lucas nodded towards her seat, the white seat that she had spent far too much time sitting in.

Once she was seated, Lucas hesitated before he stepped forward. "Please turn to the side. This is going to be a large upgrade so you will be unconscious for seven minutes. Give or take a few seconds."

Her body moved even though her mind told her not to. She hated that mechanics had so much control over her.

Slowly, he pulled the collar of her shirt down, exposing her shoulder blades. She trembled under his touch, or maybe it was his hand that was trembling. It was hard for her to tell the difference. She felt movement, heard the soft click. He gently removed a chip, set it on the counter, and replaced it with another.

Her eyes closed as her body went slack for the update. She had no idea how long she sat slumped in the chair. Eventually, the humming in her head stopped and she sat up straight. She blinked a couple of times. The mess had been cleaned up and Lucas was sitting behind his desk staring directly at her.

"Do you feel any different?" Lucas asked. It was an unusual question coming from him.

She thought about it for a moment, and shook her head. She felt the same.

She still didn't want to leave.

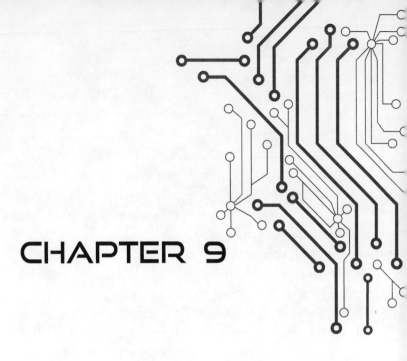

CHAPTER 9

Lucas had seen a spark of emotion in Kaitlyn's eyes. He knew he had.

He couldn't get the image out of his mind. She'd genuinely seemed upset to leave the compound. The emotion was so fleeting that for a moment he thought he'd imagined it, but it was there. He knew what he'd seen.

The lab felt colder and more silent since she'd left. Lucas sank back into his chair, his mind going over the encounter from beginning to end.

Could she possibly still have feelings after all they had done to her? It was hard for him to believe. They had overridden the signals in Kaitlyn's brain that caused any kind of human emotion. She was supposed to look human, but not possess human traits. That was the beauty of the project—or the tragedy, depending on how you looked at it.

He ran his hand through his hair, agitated. This was like his worst nightmare coming true. His justification for going along with the idea was that she wouldn't understand what they had done. She wouldn't care. When she awoke from the coma, she was supposed to have no memories of being human. In essence, they'd saved her life. She would have died from her injuries.

At least, that's what he kept telling himself.

He needed to find out the truth before they sold her off to the government. If she was harboring any kind of human thoughts or emotions, not only would she pose a threat to government security if her own moral compass affected her decision-making, but it would fall back on IFICS.

Before he could change his mind, Lucas tossed off his lab coat and grabbed his jacket from the back of his chair, jerking it on as he exited the room.

He made his way across the courtyard towards the dormitory Kaitlyn shared with the groundspeople, cooks, and other workers that lived on the compound.

He hesitated as he turned down her hallway. In all the time he had known Kaitlyn, he had never entered her bedroom. There had never been a reason to. But now....

Maybe he should just turn around. It was none of his business. He was paid to make sure she was prepared for the assignment, not to check on her emotional state of mind. Not that she had an emotional state of mind. But it kind of seemed.... The keys jingled in his hands. Screw it. He had to know.

In a few long strides, he was in front of her door. He tapped the keys lightly against the metal, thinking to himself how it was more similar to a jail cell than a bedroom.

"Yes." Kaitlyn's sweet voice floated out the door.

"Umm, it's Lucas. Is it okay if I come in for a moment?"

"Yes, you can come in."

His hands shook as he turned the key and pushed the door open.

Kaitlyn lay on her bed with her long bare legs crossed, her eyes wide and serene. The sight of her smooth, silky skin distracted him, and Lucas had to will his eyes away from her legs and to her face. He no longer noticed the teal parts of her body with the code scrolling. When he looked at Kaitlyn he saw a young woman not a machine. He felt lightheaded and almost forgot why he was there.

To divert his attention, Lucas glanced around the room. It was small, not much bigger than a closet, and everything was white. Even the curtains. Other than a little television, she didn't have anything else. She was only allowed to watch movies they deemed acceptable. Mostly spy flicks. It was mainly for her to watch humans interact outside of the locked down environment she lived in. The thought was she could pick up on mannerism and dialogue. Did she really spend all her time sitting in her room? She needed books or magazines, too. He should address the issue with the Professor. Not that it really mattered at this point. Soon she would be gone.

Kaitlyn stared blankly at him. "Can I help you?"

"Look," Lucas said, his stomach suddenly aflutter with nerves. "I'm just going to come out and say it. Can you feel things?"

She tilted her head as if trying to process the question. "Such as pain? No, I cannot."

"Not pain. Emotions. Feelings."

Kaitlyn's eyes darted to the ceiling. The red light of the camera blinked. "I don't know what you mean. You have to be more specific."

What in the world was he thinking barging into her bedroom like this? She had no clue what he was even saying.

I'm such an idiot.

Lucas sighed. "Forget it. I'm sorry, Kaitlyn. I shouldn't have bothered you."

As he turned to leave, her voice stopped him.

"Lucas, I would like some fresh air. Professor Adams says it is good for me."

The request startled him. He turned back around, meeting her blank gaze and scratched his head. "I guess I can take you outside."

"I would like to be taken outside. The fresh air is good for me." She untangled her legs and rose to her feet. Lucas watched, mesmerized, as she slid her slender feet into a pair of brown leather flats.

He held open the door, and she brushed past him. When her skin hit his, it nearly dropped him to his knees. A jolt of electricity surged through him with only the barest of touches, and he knew it wasn't because she was half electronic. A girl had never had this effect on him—and he had known a few girls. He could never seem to relate to them.

Lucas took a deep breath and steadied himself. He asked himself again what he had been thinking coming here; it was bad enough he had to see her for hours in a clinical environment. Seeing her outside of work felt more intimate, and it scared the hell out of him.

"I will show you where I walk with Quess."

"You walk with Professor Adams's granddaughter?"

"Yes."

How did he not know that? He should be talking to Quess instead of Kaitlyn. That would definitely be easier. Lucas shoved his hands deep in his pockets to stop from fidgeting as they walked the empty halls and out towards the courtyard.

It was a cool day. They didn't pass anyone on the narrow sidewalk that led away from the dormitory towards the woods. Kaitlyn broke the awkward silence. "Did you know that dogwood trees used to be called dog-tree?"

Lucas cracked a smile. "No, I wasn't aware of that fact."

"The name switched over in 1614."

"That's interesting." He slid a sideways glance to her. "Do you like dogwood trees?"

Kaitlyn looked at him blankly. "It's a tree."

His shoulders slumped an inch, disappointed. "Do you like trees?"

Lucas blinked at her in surprise. "They are needed for clean air, so yes. I like trees."

She didn't ask anything more. They continued walking, Lucas so aware of her presence beside him that he couldn't think of anything else.

They came to a large birch tree. Kaitlyn reached out and pressed her hand to the peeling bark. "This is my favorite tree."

Lucas stared up at the massive tree. She wasn't built to have preferences for something like that. He kept a straight face, trying to squash the hope that built within him. Maybe he hadn't imagined it. Maybe he really had seen emotion in her back at the lab.

"Why did you come to my room, Lucas?"

"I-I don't know. It was foolish. I'm sorry I bothered you."

"It's not a bother. I like to get out of the room."

That word again. Was she trying to tell him something?

"You do?"

Kaitlyn nodded once, a horribly robotic gesture, and kept walking. He hurried to catch up.

Lucas tried another tactic. "Kaitlyn, if I told you that you didn't have to leave, would that make you happy?"

She tried to hide it, but he saw it: a flash of hope in her wide blue eyes. "Can you do that?"

"It depends. Do you want to stay here?" He didn't have the authority to make such an offer, but he wanted to see her reaction. Maybe he could plead his case to Harrington.

Yeah, right.

She looked down at the ground and then back at Lucas. "I don't want to leave. I don't like it here, but I feel safe."

His heart rate accelerated. *Holy shit.* This was huge. Lucas wanted to run back and tell Professor Adams, but something in her face told him not to. How could he have missed the signs that she still had feelings and emotions, hopes and fears?

Lucas thought of the ramifications. Maybe he should keep this to himself. Professor Adams would want to remove any emotions, any humanity that Kaitlyn had left. He found himself wondering what her laugh sounded like. *What a strange thing to think of at a time like this.*

Kaitlyn's clear voice startled him out of his thoughts. "Do you know where they plan on sending me?"

"No. I just know it will be for a government contract."

"Will I see you again?"

Taking a deep breath, Lucas's shoulders slumped. "I hope so. Since we created you and all, I think they'll need us to stay involved." He really didn't believe that to be true, but he wished it were. The thought of never seeing her again...

"I'm going to miss you." He stiffened, surprised. Had he said that out loud?

"You are?" Kaitlyn asked, staring at him curiously. "As in feeling of loss?"

He laughed. He knew her brain analyzed words and phrases at lightning speed. "Yes, that is exactly what I meant. We've spent a lot of time together."

"Can you really help me to stay here?"

"I can try."

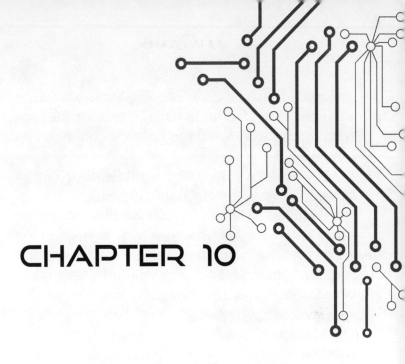

CHAPTER 10

They continued down the path into the woods. Kaitlyn couldn't believe she was alone with Lucas. How many nights had she lain awake thinking about this moment?

He looked so handsome in the fading sunlight. His coarse dark hair was sticking up in odd directions because he kept running his hand through it. Her sensors told her it was a nervous gesture, and Kaitlyn tried to dig deeper to find out if he was nervous because of her. Her sensors just flashed *No further report.*

She fought the urge to trace her fingers around the stubble on his usually clean-shaven face and press her body to his. He looked like he hadn't been sleeping well; today, he had dark circles under his beautiful eyes. She wanted to ask him if something was bothering him, but that was not something a *robot* would ask. So she continued on in silence.

It was so hard to hold up the facade, being so close and so completely alone with him.

Something inside of her wanted Lucas to know she was more than just a shell of what she used to be. Their time together was quickly coming to an end. Soon she would be sent off to who knew where. The thought of never seeing his face again left a dull ache in her chest.

Maybe she should get a check-up to see if something was wrong with her. Her body felt so different whenever he was around.

"Lucas, do you think I'm pretty?" she blurted out. *Where did that come from?*

"Excuse me?" His eyes were wide and so blue it was like looking at a cloudless day.

"I asked if you think I am pretty." The muscles in her stomach clenched. She cautiously maintained her blank expression. She had the sudden strange desire to clear her throat and look at her feet, but she didn't.

"Kaitlyn, do you really care if I think you're pretty?" He rubbed the back of his neck and stared intently at her. *Curious and confused.* The images in her scan told her.

Heat rose to her face. "Never mind. It was a stupid question. I know you think I'm just a machine in a human body."

"That's not true," he said hoarsely.

"Forget I said anything."

Kaitlyn couldn't place the sensation that arose within her. Heat filled her face and neck, and she stepped away from Lucas, unable to even look at him. She activated her scanners, searching for what was wrong with her. Was she malfunctioning?

A split-second later, her symptoms came up with a definition: humiliation.

"Kaitlyn." Lucas reached for her arm.

She took off at a run, her shoes silent on the soft grass. She wanted to get as far away from him as possible. Why would she ask such a ridiculous question? It was absurd.

"Kaitlyn! Wait up!"

She ran harder, faster, her feet pounding into the ground as she tried to put as much distance between them as possible. Trees zipped by her peripheral, and the chill wind whipped against her. The machine analyzed speed, wind direction, and counted the beat per minutes of her artificial heart, and she had no control over it whatsoever.

"Kate, please!" Lucas yelled.

She stopped in her tracks. She turned slowly, sensors working to stabilize her limbs. Lucas was running to catch up, his coat flapping behind him. His heart rate was accelerated and sweat gleamed on his forehead. Strands of his curly dark hair fell down in his left eye as he slowed his pace and thudded to a stop before her, leaning over to catch his breath. He obviously needed to work on his cardio.

"Why did you call me Kate?" she demanded.

Lucas straightened up. "I...I don't know. I've always thought you should be called Kate. Kaitlyn sounds so formal."

"I like Kate." She paused, saying the word once more in her mind. "It makes me feel strange to hear you say it."

"It does? It makes you *feel*?" Lucas said. He looked flustered, like he didn't know what to say or do.

"I don't know why." Kaitlyn kicked at the ground and looked off at the tree line. The sun was beginning to set. The sky was a beautiful shade of violet swirled through with pink. It was amazing that such beauty existed and then there was such ugliness in the world. Such as herself — not human, but not fully robot.

Lucas studied her face. "Kaitlyn, do you feel more than you let on?"

She shifted her feet and shrugged, discomfited by his gaze. "I don't know what I feel — if anything — most of the time."

"I can relate to that."

"You couldn't possibly understand what I'm going through," Kaitlyn said through gritted teeth and took a step backwards. Her vehemence surprised her; that reaction had come from somewhere deep inside.

"You're right." Lucas held up his hands. "That was insensitive and unfair. To answer your original question: You are hands down the most beautiful woman I have ever laid eyes on."

He thought she was beautiful? Kaitlyn frowned and shook her head. "You don't have to say that. I know I'm a freak."

A hurt look crossed his face. "Kate, you're not a freak. You're incredible. There is not a woman out there that could compare to you." His troubled eyes met hers. "I'm sorry we did this to you."

"You're sorry?" What did he have to be sorry about? It wasn't like it was his idea. He just worked there. If anyone was to blame, it was Harrington for coming up with the crazy notion of merging humans with machines.

"You should have had a chance to live your life without our interference." Lucas laughed, but it wasn't in humor. Kaitlyn's sensors supplied a definition for 'irony.' "Kate, you're amazing. You are beautiful, and the person you were... We took that from you."

"Lucas, look at me!" Kaitlyn said, lifting the hem of her shirt to her bra line. "I have so many chips implanted in me that I don't know where I start and where the machine begins. Scars cover my body, and not to mention this." Kaitlyn pointed at the translucent part of her arm. The patches of see-through plastic were spread over various parts of her body. "How could you possibly think I'm beautiful? I'm repulsive—a freak of nature."

A strange sensation on her face gave her pause. She reached up and touched her cheek, then drew wet fingertips away.

What...was that a tear?

Her artificial heart pounded in her ears as she stared at her hand, captivated. After all the time she had spent at the facility, all she had been through, she'd never cried. She didn't think she could.

Across from her, Lucas stared. "Oh my God. Kate."

She didn't know what to say, so she just lifted her hand and murmured, "I'm...crying."

Lucas grabbed her hand, the wetness of her tears smeared on her skin as he closed the space between them. He pressed his forehead to hers. Her mind screamed at her to run, but her body was rooted in place. She was so confused by the way he made her feel. His closeness was exhilarating and terrifying at the same time.

"Kate, I'm so sorry. I didn't know." His thumb gently rubbed another tear away, making her shiver.

"Didn't know what?" She sniffled, and then berated herself for showing weakness. Now that he knew her secret...

"That you could feel."

"Why does it matter? Are you going to bring me back to the lab and erase what is left of me?"

"No, Kate. We've done all the programming we know how as far as emotions go. In truth, it's amazing. Goes to show how incredible the human mind is."

"It's only you that makes me feel things. Well, I guess Quess too. I like her."

Lucas stared at her for a moment. "No one else?"

She shook her head and looked away.

"Do you feel the same for me as you do for Quess?"

"Definitely not. I like Quess as a friend."

"And me?"

"You make my body feel like it's revving up when I am standing still. I don't know how to describe it. I wake up looking forward to seeing you and I go to bed thinking of you." Kate quietly.

Lucas took a step forward, and he leaned down and pressed his lips gently to hers.

Kaitlyn froze, unsure how to react. She had pictured this many times, but now that it was happening her body felt like it was going into overdrive. His firm lips pressed harder to hers, and she parted her own. She wanted to taste him. She wanted to crawl into his body and never leave. Just one kiss, and she felt like the world had dropped from beneath her.

She could feel his heart beating in his chest. Heart rate: one hundred and twenty. Much too high for a non-physical activity.

Kaitlyn pulled away, his mint and cinnamon taste on her lips. "Lucas, are you sick? Your heart rate is so high."

He smiled faintly. "That's what you do to me."

Alarmed, Kaitlyn touched his chest. "I did this to you?"

"It's okay, Kate." Lucas pushed a strand of her hair behind her ear. The touch of his hand made her tremble inside. "You drive me crazy. Being this close to you. I can't explain it. I've dreamed about this moment. No one has ever had this effect on me. Ever."

Kaitlyn stiffened at the word 'dreamed.' The blond haired guy flashed in her mind. Who was he? *Who cares?* All she wanted was Lucas.

Her body melted to his. The warmth of his skin against hers was almost too much to bear. Could he really want her the way she wanted him? Her hands ached to explore every part of his body. She wanted to know him from the inside out.

His mouth made its way down her neck, causing her to go into sensory overload. She couldn't concentrate or think; all she could do was feel. It was amazing. He calmed all the random thoughts, the analysis, definitions and patterns that intruded on her thoughts. There was no analyzing, no patterns, and no past; there was only now.

"Lucas." His name escaped from her lips on a gasp.

He made his way back up, and his lips met hers. His kiss was filled with urgency, and she felt like she was going to spin out of control. Her breath caught in her throat. How could a kiss take her breath away? The effect he had on her wasn't rational, but she gave in to it anyway. He made her feel alive.

When he pulled away, his eyes searched hers. "What are we going to do?" Lucas asked.

Instantly, her mind ran through the scenarios. None of them looked positive. She shook her head, unable to answer. She wasn't even sure what he meant. Was he talking about the kiss, her feelings or her leaving soon?

"We'll figure something out." His words sounded hollow. They both knew nothing good would come out of the situation.

She was too vital to Harrington for him to let her go.

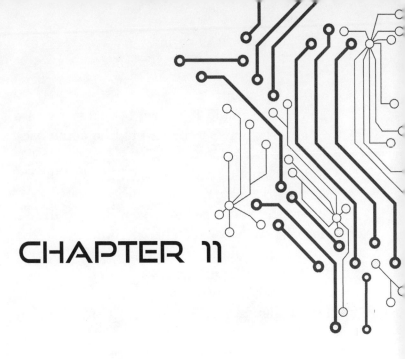

CHAPTER 11

The dorm room door closed softly behind her, locking automatically. It took so much self-control to stop the grin from spreading across her face.

She didn't know it was possible to feel this alive. This *happy*. Lucas was responsible for the emotions; she knew that with absolute certainty. If she had known it would be like this she would have told him long ago how she felt about him.

But soon she would leave. The thought hit her hard. Panic rose within her, but it was quickly overridden by her sensors that sent signals to her microprocessor. The familiar hum washed over her body, steadying her. It was strange—when there was distance between them, her body could manage the reaction, but when he was near, she seemed to lose control.

Before she made it to her bed, there was a knock at her door. She froze. Had he come back for her? No, it was Quess.

Kaitlyn smoothed down her dress and turned to face the doorway. "Come in."

When the door opened, Quess hurried inside, her face lit with excitement. "I came by earlier and you weren't here. Where were you?"

"I took a walk with Lucas."

"You what? Are you serious?" Quess sputtered, her jaw falling open. "How did that happen?"

Kaitlyn kept her face impassive, even though she wanted to tell Quess everything. The thought of smashing the camera crossed her mind, but she pushed it aside. Instead, Kaitlyn motioned to the camera with her eyes. "He needed to ask me some questions to make sure my programming was working correctly."

Quess looked up at the flashing dot, and then back at Kaitlyn. "Well, now you need to go for a walk with *me*—now. My grandfather sent me." She spoke a little too loudly, as if for the benefit of the cameras.

"Okay." Kaitlyn walked towards the door, exchanging a look with her friend as she passed.

They made their way down the long corridor as classical music streamed from the speakers above them. There were two women standing in front of the exit.

"Hey." Quess waved and smiled. One of the women gave a strained smile and the other avoided looking at them. As if the top of her shoes were more interesting. Seemed to be the normal reaction of most of the staff when they saw Kaitlyn.

They moved aside to allow them to pass. Quess pushed open the door and the stepped into shadows. Darkness was starting to fall. A misty yellow glare from the security lights illuminated the grounds as they flicked on in the twilight.

Quess walked as fast as her legs would take her towards their safe zone, the place where Kaitlyn had taken Lucas. Kaitlyn wondered what had her friend so excited. Usually it was a new dress she wanted to tell her about, or that her Nanny had made special cookies. Everything seemed to make the girl excited.

When they finally reached the birch tree, Quess squealed, "I was right – he was on Facebook. I found him."

"You did?" Kaitlyn asked, surprised. "Are you sure it's him?"

"Yes, I'm sure. His name is Evan. He's twenty-one, has a labrador retriever named Spike, two younger sisters—you know the type— cheerleaders, and his parents divorced when he was twelve. He's very hot, like on fire."

Kaitlyn's mind whirled as she grasped what

Quess was saying. She wasn't quite sure what to make of this news. On the one hand, she was curious, but on the other hand, there was Lucas. He was her reality now.

"That's impressive, Quess. How do you know all of this?"

"I told you. Facebook. It's like a peek into someone's private world."

"But… On fire? Twenty-one?" Kaitlyn asked, her mind sorting through the information.

Quess smiled sheepishly. "He's not really on fire—as in flames. He's sexy. That's what I mean."

"Oh."

"That's not all…"

"Well, then tell me the rest."

"There are tons of pictures of you on there."

Kaitlyn froze. "Me?"

"You looked so happy." Quess said thoughtfully. "Although, I have to say your taste in clothing—not so great."

Kaitlyn suddenly felt lightheaded. The woods began to spin in her vision. Was her processor shorting?

She heard a muffled, "Kaitlyn, are you alright?"

Next thing she knew, there was only darkness.

Someone was shaking her.

"Kaitlyn. Please wake up." Quess's voice was panicked.

Kaitlyn's eyes fluttered open, and she squinted. Why was she on the ground? Her head felt heavier than usual as she glanced around, her eyes quickly adjusting.

"I'm okay." Kaitlyn pushed herself to a sitting position, using a nearby tree to lean against. She was lucky she didn't fall into it when she passed out.

"What happened?" Quess asked, her eyes concerned.

"I don't know."

"We should take you to see my grandfather."

"No. I'm fine." Then it came back to her what they were talking about when she passed out...or when her body shut down. She wasn't sure if there was a difference. "Please, don't tell him."

Quess nodded. "Whatever you want."

Kaitlyn accessed her memory files and sorted through her thoughts from their previous conversation. "I believe you mentioning details about my past caused me to shut down. That must be it."

"Like a safety measure or something?" Quess sat on the grass and pulled her knees to her chest.

"I just need a moment." Kaitlyn closed her eyes and waited until she felt normal again. Her rhythms settled into familiar patterns. The mechanisms in place had been successful. Whatever happened had passed. Was it possible the IFICS had somehow connected her real memories to some kind of fail-safe blocking system? "I'm fine now. Tell me what else you saw." She paused. "But don't use their names. Just in case that was the trigger for my shut down."

Quess nodded in understanding. The girl had a quick mind. She paused as if trying to compose her words carefully before she spoke them.

"There was this girl who passed away, and everyone she went to school with was devastated, but mostly her boyfriend. He started a memorial page in her honor. He posted pictures of them together all over it, and her friends did, too. To this day, they even comment and tell her happy birthday. Like a shrine. Her boyfriend wasn't able to move on without her. It was sweet, but also a bit strange."

"Where was she from?"

"Near the ocean."

Kaitlyn wanted to ask so many questions, but was afraid it would make her black out again.

"Kaitlyn!" a voice in the distance yelled.

Kaitlyn jumped to her feet and looked around. Her sensors analyzed the voice patterns. It was Lucas, and he was over two hundred meters away, but moving quickly. His voice sounded strained, out of breath.

A few moments later, he came into view. "There you are. Thank goodness. We got an alert that one of your sensor's shorted out."

"I'm okay. I felt funny and then sort of shut down."

His eyes searched hers. "What were you doing at the time?"

"Just talking to Quess."

Lucas narrowed his eyes and looked at Quess. "What were you talking about?"

"It's not important," Kaitlyn said a little too sharply.

"The hell it isn't."

"What, you don't monitor what she says?" Quess jumped up and put her hands on her narrow hips. "You have cameras all over the place. I kinda figured you knew every word she said before she said it."

"It's not like that," Lucas said flatly. Kaitlyn noted that there wasn't much conviction in his tone. His blue eyes turned back to Kaitlyn. "Kate. Please tell me what you were talking about. We need to figure this out. There must be a glitch somewhere, and we need to have it straightened out before your unveiling."

"Right. We can't have your precious project breaking down, can we?" Kaitlyn said coldly. Of course, that was more important to him. Did the kiss they shared mean anything to him?

"Kate, there are ways we can find out, but I don't think you want us to do that, do you? Professor Adams will also have been alerted to the shutdown. He's probably already at the lab scrambling to figure out what went wrong."

Her body stiffened. She knew he was right. They could give her truth serum drugs, maybe somehow go into her history file data. Or worse.

"Fine, we were just talking about my past. Happy?"

"Your past?" Lucas raised an eyebrow. "Exactly what about your past? What do you know about it?"

Kaitlyn hesitated. She didn't want to give up information on the man from her dreams, especially after hearing what Quess had found out about him and the 'shrine'. Even after all this time, he hadn't let go.

And regardless of the kiss, Lucas's main concern was clearly the project.

"I was telling Quess that I've been having dreams about the ocean."

"The ocean? That's it?"

"Yes. Dreams of me swimming in the ocean. Why would that cause me to short circuit?"

Lucas ran his hand down his jaw line and looked away, lost in thought. "Are you sure there isn't more? I don't see why that would have caused you to short out. Have any other memories surfaced?"

"I have no memories, Lucas. You and Professor Adams took care of that."

He stared at her for a long time before finally conceding. "Maybe it was just a random glitch.

We'll do more testing in the morning."

"Of course you will," Quess spat. "That's all you do to her. Why can't you just leave her alone?"

A look of hurt crossed his beautiful face. "Let's get you both back to the dormitory. Quess, I don't know if it's a good idea that you spend time with Kaitlyn anymore."

Quess glared at him. "Well, good thing that's not up to you."

Kaitlyn gave her friend a comforting look, and then took Lucas by the arm, leading him away from her friend. She leaned forward, speaking quietly. "Lucas, please don't take Quess away from me. She's the only person that talks to me. I promise I won't bring up anything about my past again. Just don't take her away."

His eyes softened. "I'll see what I can do."

"Thank you." She wanted to throw her arms around him, but that would not be appropriate behavior. Her mind raced. So much had taken place in such a short amount of time. She wasn't sure how she felt about the new information regarding her past, or what was going on between her and Lucas.

If anything.

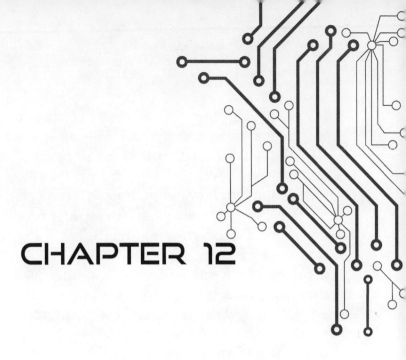

CHAPTER 12

They screwed up. Somehow, they screwed up.

"How is this even possible?" Lucas muttered to himself as entered the dimly building.

Not only was Kaitlyn exhibiting emotions, she was experiencing memories. Neither should have slipped through the robot's overrides. He couldn't believe the way she had kissed him. He had never felt so wanted or needed in his life. If anyone felt emotions, it was Kate.

But what if her feelings got in the way of her job? She was designed for a very specific purpose, and that did *not* involve forming emotional connections. That switch should be firmly in the off position. She should be able to do anything asked of her without question or fear.

This is not good.

Lucas shoved open the door to his office, a closet-sized space tucked into a corner near the lab. The thought struck him that the purpose of her very existence was to be put in harm's way. He hated it. And now, with human emotions leaking into her consciousness, it could prove even more of a danger for Kaitlyn. What if she hesitated on a job and it got her killed?

Lucas took long strides to his computer and the chair squeaked noisily as he sank into it. He pulled up Kaitlyn's files on the computer. *Harrington will flip when he finds out.*

Lucas started carefully reading through each line of code—coding that he had written—looking for the answer.

After four hours, his eyes were blurring from looking at the numbers for so long. Maybe there *wasn't* a way to turn off emotions, and they had just been fooling themselves all along. Wishful thinking. There had to be a scientific explanation.

And then he saw it. His heart fell. *No. No. No. This can't be.*

He never made mistakes, but there it was. One number wrong, and the entire sequence was faulty. It was an easy fix. *Damn it!* What the hell was he going to do? A couple of strokes on the keyboard, and a new upgrade, and Kaitlyn would be *fixed*. Emotionless and good as new. She would never look at him with that longing, that same intensity again.

He slumped in his chair, and rubbed his face. As crazy as it sounded, he knew he had fallen in love with Kaitlyn. It had happened gradually—all the days they'd spent together, alone, testing her skills; all the times he'd admired her strength and endurance. He'd fought against it for so long, thinking he was an idiot for essentially falling in love with a robot. A non-human. But there was no denying his feelings now that she returned them. She wasn't a robot, after all. She was real.

She was always on his mind, and to know it was mutual... How could he erase that? He stared at the code across the screen, the flashing cursor set at the glaring mistake. He had naively hoped the coding was correct, and her feelings for him had overridden the computer somehow, like one of those cheesy romantic movies. He had hoped that a small part of her had remained, and that part wanted him.

But her desire for him had been nothing more than a slip of a keystroke.

Lucas had a sudden urge to throw the computer across the room. Instead, he closed his eyes and breathed deeply.

He had to get a grip. The project came first. That was what he was paid for—to make sure she was the sleekest, fittest, strongest, most intelligent mechanical soldier on the planet. Her life depended on it.

He had to do it. He couldn't risk her being dismantled because he selfishly wanted her for himself. As much as it pained him, he knew what he had to do. It was the only choice he had — the right choice.

But for who?

If only he could have one more night with her. If only he could put off fixing the coding until the day after tomorrow…

No, he had to do it now. If he spent another day with her, he knew he might not be strong enough to fix her at all

His fingers hesitated over the keyboard. He pictured her beautiful face, and the excitement in her unusual grey eyes. At least *he* would have the memory of their evening together. She would have nothing.

It's for the best.

Before he could change his mind, he made the correction and watched as the coding scrolled down the computer screen, updating her system commands. He inserted the new chip and waited for the data to transfer. Tomorrow, he would implant the new chip, and she would be a true cyborg. The thought made Lucas sick to his stomach. He was a monster.

All in the name of science.

The next morning, Kaitlyn walked into the lab wearing nothing but a stark white hospital gown, her feet bare. Lucas noted that she avoided eye contact with everyone in the room as she walked over and sat on the cold steel table, and waited. Her hands rested lightly on the edge of the table, and her feet hung motionless. The nurse rushed over and withdrew her blood, and then quickly left the room.

His heart sank. Without a word he moved away from Professor Adams, and made his way to his desk to pick up the upgrade chip. Watching Kaitlyn from the corner of his eye.

He knew now that her fluid movements, her blank stare, it was all an act. He couldn't imagine what she had been going through all this time, sitting motionless, expressionless, in front of them. In front of the cameras. Her level of self-control was impressive. At least he could take comfort in the fact that he would be removing the mental anguish she must have been dealing with every day.

Sure, Lucas. Keep telling yourself that. He clenched his fists at his side, tempted to put them both through the nearest window. A little pain and blood could clear his mind and take away his frustration over what was about to happen. The removal of the only spark of life she had left. He opened his right hand and stared down at the tiny, innocuous chip, and crossed the room towards her. He had to do it. In two days, they would hand her over to the Department of

Defense. He inhaled deeply, steeling himself.

"Kaitlyn. We're going to give you another upgrade that should avoid another shut down," he said. "We're also implanting the slang chip so conversations will be easier for you to follow, as well as a facial recognition program that will give you the ability to tell what people are thinking and feeling by their expressions. I'm sure you've picked up a lot on your own through watching others interact, but this will make it easier. You are programmed to be very adaptable. Eventually, you will be able to mimic them on your own during interaction."

I'm also going to take away any feelings you had for me. He groaned inwardly.

She nodded her head slightly in acknowledgement. Her eyes met his there wasn't a hint of distrust in her grey eyes. Which made it even worse.

It was killing him. He forced his breathing to slow and tried to quiet the emotions raging in his mind. She trusted him completely. If she knew what he was about to do, he knew she would beg him not to, and he would be helpless to tell her no.

His hand shook as he walked around behind her and gently untied the top of the hospital gown to expose the plastic and metal door in the center of her back. He opened the plastic on her back. The skin on either side was smooth, completely unmarred by anything but the transparent teal door. With a click, Lucas disconnected and removed the old processor chip and implanted the new one, wondering if she would feel the changes. Probably not.

He closed the plastic door again and it slotted into place. His hand lingered on her skin longer than necessary. Being so close to her was too much. He closed his eyes and took a deep breath. Her processor was updating as he watched. He had just ended any chance he had of a real relationship with her, the one woman he wanted. He had never connected to another woman the way he did Kaitlyn. Sure, he'd had a couple of girlfriends—sexual partners, really—but they had never meant anything of significance to him.

Maybe he was meant to be alone. He deserved to be alone after what they–he–had done to Kate.

He cleared his throat. "I have to go take care of some things," Lucas said as he pulled his hand away.

Kaitlyn didn't reply. Her body had slumped slightly forward, and she could not even hear him.

He lied. There was nothing he had to do, but he couldn't stand being in the same room as her, knowing what he had done. It was like she was his mirror and he couldn't stand to look at his own reflection. He grabbed his coat and rushed out of the room without another word—leaving Kaitlyn all alone.

What a coward, he thought, disgusted with himself.

He didn't deserve her.

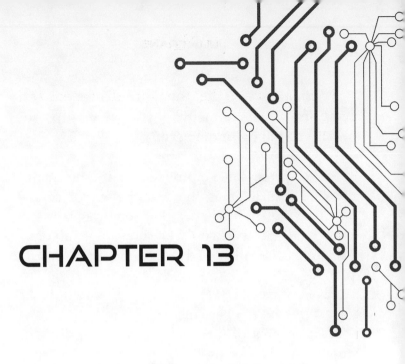

CHAPTER 13

Lucas walked out of the lab, passing Adams on his way in. The professor greeted him, but Lucas didn't respond.

Odd, Kaitlyn thought as the door clicked shut behind Lucas.

She didn't feel any different, but that wasn't a surprise. She could rarely tell when they made changes these days. The little tweaks were not as jarring as the big upgrades in the beginning had been. Everything they did now was to make her more efficient. More of a machine.

"Kaitlyn, I do believe you've received your last upgrade." Adams said with a smile. He scribbled something unintelligible on the white board as he spoke.

"The last?"

"Yes, unless something else comes up. You should be ready for delivery."

"Delivery?"

The professor continued as if she hadn't spoken. "As long as they want you, of course. There is the slight chance that they might not be interested, but that would be shocking to all of us. You are the most advanced human on the planet."

Human — yeah, right.

"Where will I be sent?"

The professor turned to stare at her. "Well, I guess there is no sense in keeping it a secret, since you are the one that will be going. I've heard rumors of a top secret facility for special projects such as yourself."

"There are others?" Kaitlyn kept her voice neutral. This was the longest conversation she had ever had with the professor.

He laughed. "No, not like you. Not yet anyway. Mostly drones and other robotic equipment that they use on the black side."

"Black side?"

"Yes, secret. No budget. No paper trail. Things that exist in a void."

Being in a void didn't sound too appealing, but like usual she kept her thoughts to herself.

Kaitlyn's body went into alert mode and a giant yellow 'Caution' flashed in her vision.

Someone was approaching the lab from the hallway. Her every muscle tensed, preparing for action. Moments later, the door swung open.

The man who entered was easily categorized by Kaitlyn's machinery: six foot two, two hundred fifteen pounds, jet black hair greying at the temples, and sharp blue-grey eyes. His face was weathered, but he aged well. Current age — sixty-three.

With mechanical precision, Kaitlyn locked gazes with the man. She had to fight the urge to jump up and wrap her hands around Dr. Harrington's throat. She was programmed to observe any subjects with a 'caution' categorization, but not act until it elevated to a 'warning'. Her body felt odd, and she quickly analyzed the feeling as rage.

That's new.

Her analyzers began listing the many ways she could kill Harrington, but then logic took over. If she killed him, it wouldn't do her any good; they would probably deactivate and disassemble her. Disassembly didn't sound good. Her body would die. There was not enough human to survive without the help from the computers. As much as she disliked her new life, she wasn't ready to cease to exist.

It had been sixty-four days since she had last seen her creator, Matthew Harrington, owner and founder of IFICS. He carried his large body with athletic grace, and he looked the same, except his skin was a shade or two darker. She should have warned him that too much sun exposure was dangerous, but she kept her mouth closed.

"Professor. Is the subject ready?" the man said in a smooth, deep voice, not taking his eyes off Kaitlyn.

"Dr. Harrington." The professor held out his hand and clasped Harrington's hand in his own. "So nice of you to drop by. Yes, the subject is more than ready. Magnificent piece of work, if I do say so myself. She is going to stun on her unveiling."

"As she should. We only have four days until we meet with the committee."

"I'm sure they will be pleased. Quite pleased indeed." Professor Adams shifted uneasily. Kaitlyn zoomed in on his face and the word 'nervous' flashed across her field of vision. Recalling his behavior sixty-four days ago, she concluded that he always looked that way when Harrington was onsite. Kaitlyn didn't understand why. Adams was only the brains behind the operation, Harrington just supplied the cash and took the credit. At least, that was what she had been able to gather during the time she had been awake and alert. After her body healed from the accident and the upgrades.

"They better be pleased," Harrington said sharply and turned his attention back to Kaitlyn.

"We have everything riding on this."

Dr. Harrington was clearly a man used to getting his way. 'Arrogant prick' ran through her head. She had to analyze it for a moment to realize it was part of her upgrade. *Interesting*. So prick had two *completely* different meanings...

Harrington crossed the room until he was standing only inches from her. Armani suit, bronze Panerai dive watch, Clive Christian cologne—$375 a bottle, and Barker Black shoes. Nothing but the best.

He ran his hand down the side of her face and trailed it all the way down the side of her arm. His skin was warm against hers. "It's going to be so hard to give you away. You are my life's work. I've dreamed of creating you since I was a little boy." Her sensors informed her that his expression was sincere, as if he indeed was making a great sacrifice. If that was true, then why did he have to give her away?

Not a threat.

Her body relaxed.

She said nothing. She only answered him if he asked a question, which he rarely did.

Harrington's blue-grey eyes stared into her own. "It has to be done. You are the future of mankind. It still pisses me off I'm going to have to hand you over to someone else. It's like giving away my first born."

She had no idea what that meant. The

thought of leaving what had become her home sent her reeling. She shouldn't have cared where they put her, but leaving one owner for another was frightening. Not to mention never seeing Lucas or Quess again. Her body revved up, and then cooled down just as quickly. No one was the wiser.

Just then, Lucas returned through the double doors. His blue eyes searched her face as if looking for something. His shoulders slumped, and his eyes appeared weary. "Dr. Harrington, hello," Lucas said, shifting his attention to where it belonged.

Harrington crossed the room to meet him. He threw his arm around Lucas's shoulder. "My dear boy, we did it." The old man's face broke into a huge grin, and Harrington stared at Kaitlyn, full of pride. Standing side by side, the two men looked as if they could be related.

"Fill me in on her upgrades," Harrington said to Lucas as they walked out the door without another word to Kaitlyn or Professor Adams.

She could hear them talking until they made it down the hallway and out the exit door. Lucas did not mention their conversation from the night before to Dr. Harrington. At least, not yet. He had promised he would keep it to himself.

She hoped he was a man of his word. Something in her told her he could be trusted. Much like Quess and her pinky promise.

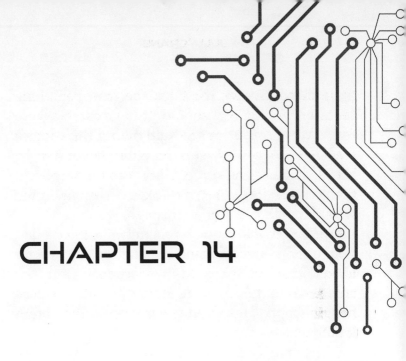

CHAPTER 14

Lucas sat at his desk, tapping his foot. He was the only one left in the lab; everyone else had gone home. There was a reason for that, beyond his usual overworked, overachieving ways: He was dying to see Kaitlyn—alone.

He wanted to make sure, to see for himself that the upgrade worked, even though the confirmation would tear him apart.

What he needed was a legitimate excuse to go back to her room. He looked around the office and grabbed a folder off the desk. It would have to do. He'd make something up if he was stopped, not that they would, the guards usually left him alone. With Harrington back, however, he'd rather play it safe.

He hurried out the door and down the long hallway.

He was anxious to see Kaitlyn, but there was a twinge of fear in his chest. He didn't know if he could handle the probability of a completely blank stare. Seeing her look at him like that would be like a bullet through his heart. *Self-inflicted.* Would she remember what had happened between them last night? The coding should not have erased the memory, but she could be confused by it, or just write it off as insignificant. He wasn't sure how her brain would access the information.

She hadn't acknowledged him all day, not that she'd really had the opportunity. If she was still in there she would have found a way to let him know. A glance, anything, but she had been robotic all day.

As he turned down the J-shaped hallway that led into the dormitories, his step faltered. A janitor stood in the middle of the walkway, pushing a broom. The older gentleman glanced up and acknowledged Lucas with a tip of his hat.

"Evening," Lucas responded, sidestepping around the man and clutching his folder. Nothing more was said, and Lucas left the janitor behind, the sound of the steady swish of the broom fading the further he walked. When he finally stood in front of her door, he closed his eyes and took a deep, calming breath.

Before he had a chance to knock, her voice filtered through the door. "Come in, Lucas."

Of course she knew he was coming. She most likely knew before he made it down the second hallway. It was one of the things she was programmed to do. She could detect motion and potential threats. Her mind filtered sounds at an unprecedented rate, and her body was always on alert.

They key scraped the lock and Lucas pushed open the door. His body was tensed.

Kaitlyn was sitting on the edge of her bed with her feet planted on the floor, staring straight ahead. The TV was on and she was watching a National Geographic documentary turned down low. She reached for the remote and clicked it off. Lucas rubbed his arms as goose pimples formed on his skin; the room was cold—colder than would be bearable for a normal human, though Kaitlyn's thin cotton dress showed she was unbothered by it.

"Kaitlyn, would you come with me for a walk? I'd like to ask you some questions." He opened the folder to punctuate his statement, but closed it quickly when he realized there was nothing in it. *Smooth.*

"Okay." Kaitlyn stood up and smoothed her dress down before slipping into her shoes.

Lucas fought the urge to tell her to grab a jacket, that it was cold outside. It stung him that he so often gave her human characteristics; he wanted her to be fully human. To react to the weather. He had never seen her shiver.

"How are you feeling?" he asked as he held the door open. She slid past him, causing him to inhale sharply as her skin touched his. Even though he knew she could no longer feel for him, she still tied him up in knots. He would probably never get over her. And he had done it to himself. That was the worst part.

This was not going to be easy.

Kaitlyn inclined her head. "I'm fine. Thank you."

Lucas was at a loss for words as they made their way outside. The sun was dipping below the horizon, low enough that the sidewalk lights had already flickered on. The fragrant smell of a burning fireplace filled the chilled evening air. He glanced sidelong at her, hoping for a response to the cold, but she just fell into step beside him, her arms hanging loosely at her sides.

"Do you like the new upgrades?" Lucas tilted his head to the left to see her clearly.

"They are interesting. The slang chip and the facial recognition will be very useful. Humans express so much with their faces," Kaitlyn responded stoically looking up at him briefly. "Sixty to seventy percent of meaning is derived from nonverbal behavior in communication. I think I'll understand people better now." Her gaze carefully scanned the perimeter.

Lucas knew she was looking for threats. As she was programmed. He flinched at the reference to 'humans.'

"Like now," she spoke up again, her grey eyes moving to settle on his face. "You flinched. I know it bothers you when I say humans. I wouldn't have picked that up before."

"We should have thought of adding the program sooner."

"I agree. I didn't realize so many words had double meanings."

They drew near to Kaitlyn's favorite tree. He wondered if she would notice the sturdy birch today. The new chip should have removed that preference from her mind.

Lucas realized he had a lot in common with the tree. Kate shouldn't be attracted to him and yet she *had* been.

She didn't say anything as they passed the large tree.

A wave of sadness washed over him; the old Kaitlyn was gone.

"Can we go that way?" She pointed off to the right where a slant-roofed gardner's shed sat illuminated by a security light.

"Of course." Lucas was puzzled that she would want to change direction. Maybe her sensors had picked up on something in that area.

Once they reached a large oak tree, Kaitlyn sat down and shifted to the side to make room for him.

After a slight hesitation, Lucas sank down to the ground beside her. He braced himself for the cold, distant Kaitlyn. Her knee brushed his and sent a jolt through him. He longed to touch her, to lean over and capture her lips again and feel her warmth, but he kept his hands by his side. He would have to live with his decision. His unhappiness for the sake of the project. Dear God, what had he become?

"What did you want to ask me?" Kaitlyn asked, her palms resting lightly on her thighs. In the twilight, her legs looked long and pale.

Lucas flushed. "Oh. Umm, I just kinda made that up. I wanted to see you."

"I was hoping you would come by."

"You were?" he said, surprised. He hadn't been expecting that at all.

She nodded and cast her grey eyes upward to meet his. The moment their gazes met, he felt like he was falling.

He couldn't stop himself; it was as if she was pulling him towards her, drawing him in. Next thing he knew, his lips were crashing down on hers, and her arms were behind his head, pulling him closer. His eyes widened in surprise, and he dropped the folder. She was soft and pliant beneath his hands, her mouth moving against his, timid, and then needy.

She's still in there—but that's impossible.

All thought left his mind, and he closed his eyes, allowing his body to relax into hers. Nothing had ever felt so right in his life even though he knew it was so wrong.

He broke away gasping. This wasn't possible. She shouldn't be acting like this. He had fixed the coding personally. "Kate…"

"Why did you stop?" she gasped, curling her fingers into his shirt as if going to pull him back.

Lucas dropped his hands from her shoulders and tried to gather his thoughts. "What do you feel for me?"

"I-I don't know. I like the way you make me feel when you kiss me. Everything fades away, and it's just us. My mind calms."

"Is that the same way you felt yesterday?"

"Yes. Why are you asking these questions? Do you not want to kiss me?"

"What?" Lucas couldn't help the laugh that burst from him. He traced a palm down her cheek. "No, it's not that. I want to kiss you more than I've ever wanted anything before in my life. It just doesn't make sense. You shouldn't have emotions towards me. You shouldn't have emotions *at all*. You weren't programmed that way."

As soon as the words slipped out of his mouth, he wished he could take them back.

Her face went still, as if a mask had dropped

down. "You're right. I wasn't programmed that way."

"Kate, please..." he said, "you don't understand. Yesterday, I found out there was an error in your coding that would leave you vulnerable to forming attachments. Forming attachments like...but I fixed it. So this can't be. It shouldn't be possible."

He knew her mind was whirring, processing the information. There was a certain look to her eyes when it happened. Maybe nobody but Lucas could tell, and only because he had studied her for so long—and not just as a robot.

"You fixed me?" she asked coldly.

"I didn't mean it that way. I meant I fixed the coding. If you still feel this way, it's amazing. It's astounding...." He shoved a hand through his hair, trying to pick his words. "It shouldn't be, but it is. There's more to it than coding, here."

"So when you 'fixed' me," Kaitlyn said, as if he hadn't spoken, "I was no longer supposed to be attracted to you?"

Lucas paused to take a deep breath. "That's what I expected, yeah."

"And you did it anyway?" Her grey eyes flashed with anger and her jaw tightened.

Oh shit, she's pissed. He scrambled to think of the words to right the situation. "You don't understand. I did it for you."

Her voice raised. "For me?"

"Yes, it could be a liability when you leave here. I couldn't stand the risk of you getting hurt."

"So you wanted to take away what little feelings I had left? What little there was of my humanity?"

Lucas looked down at the ground, shame settling over him.

"Well I'm sorry to inform you, but it didn't work." She moved to stand up, and Lucas grabbed her arm.

"Kate, please just hear me out. You're leaving in a couple of days. I don't know if we will see each other again. Do you really want to waste what little time we have left together arguing? I'm begging you. Please, I was an idiot, but I really thought I was doing what was best for you.""

She pulled her hand away and stared at him. Several emotions flashed across her face. Lucas saw the moment logic took over her thought processes, and her grey eyes softened. He was thankful she was able to see the situation objectively. Even though she was clearly upset only a moment ago. If she never talked to him again he would never forgive himself.

One dainty, long-fingered hand flitted to rest on his arm. Lucas stood up to tentatively pulled her towards him. When she didn't resist his shoulders relaxed.

"As much as I hate to admit it, I can comprehend why you would think it was a good idea. But you should have asked me first. I deserve a choice. You took that away from me. You can't imagine what it's like having others make ever decision for you."

"You're right. I should have talked it over with you. I'm sorry. I really am."

"So, I shouldn't have feelings for you, but I do. What does that mean?" Kaitlyn pulled back to look up at him.

His lip twitched. "That I'm irresistible?" He looked away, bashful. *That was so lame.*

"It does seem that way, doesn't it?" She looked pensive. "I guess I don't understand why they don't want me to have feelings or emotions. There are soldiers everyday that do their jobs well, and they have families and people they care about."

"You're not supposed to be any old soldier, though," Lucas said. "You are supposed to surpass the best soldier. And emotions get in the way." Lucas touched her cheek; her skin was warm.

There was a long silence before she spoke again. "Are you going to tell Professor Adams?"

Lucas stuck his hands deep in his pockets and looked off in the distance at the towering trees. The sun was gone completely; night had fallen. He knew he should tell the professor. "Not unless you want me to. As far as I'm concerned, the coding is correct. I did my part, and you have done a convincing job of fooling everyone."

"I don't want you to tell them." She held out her pinky.

"You learned that from Quess?" He laughed.

She nodded and waited. Lucas held out his own hand, so much larger than hers. They hooked pinky fingers, and shook.

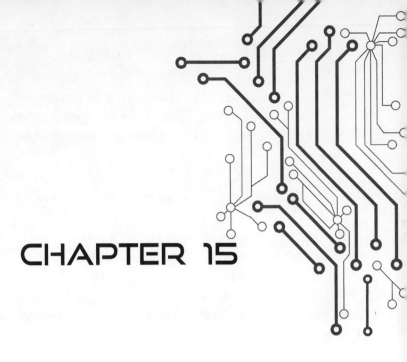

CHAPTER 15

Kaitlyn sank to the ground, pulling Lucas with her, and rested against the tree. She felt better after their pinky promise. She had to admit she was a little relieved to know that the feelings for Lucas were real, and not a computing error.

Lucas opened his arms and tugged her close. She rested her head against his chest and listened to the steady rhythm of his heart. Even in the cool evening she could feel the warmth of his skin through his clothes.

She should have been angry with Lucas, but being with him felt so right. She didn't want to squander away the short amount of time they had together not getting along. The thought of never seeing him again sent a brief wave of panic through her that her systems quickly overrode.

"What were you like when you were younger?" Kaitlyn asked, lifting her face to peer up at him.

"I can't believe you still want to be with me," Lucas said softly and ran his thumb slowly across her lower lip. "I thought I'd lost you forever."

"That feels good." Kaitlyn closed her eyes at the touch of his hand.

"How about this?" Lucas's warm breath on her neck caused her to gasp as he flipped her hair off her shoulder and lightly kissed from her collarbone to her temple.

"That, too."

His lips moved across the sensitive skin at the base of her neck, his tongue darting out to touch her. She shuddered, one hand reaching up to cup his face and draw him closer.

His touch was intoxicating; it set her blood boiling, flushing her body with heat. Kaitlyn completely lost herself when he was so near. "Kiss me," she whispered.

His lips met hers, slowly exploring with an urgency that left her breathless.

Eventually, she pulled away and met his gaze. "Are you distracting me with pleasure to avoid my question?"

Lucas laughed, long and hard, his body shaking beneath her touch. He leaned forward, kissing her again, just a short, affectionate peck.

"You're too astute."

Kaitlyn straightened up, putting some breathing room between them. She cupped his face and looked him in the eye. "Tell me about your childhood. We don't have much time together, and I want to know more about your past. I hardly know anything about you."

"Let's just say I'm glad you didn't know me when I was younger." He tugged on a lock of her hair, but his eyes were dark and sad.

"Why?"

"Well, I was what one would call a 'nerd.' Tall, lanky, no social skills, and eye glasses as thick as a coke bottle."

Kaitlyn tried to match the mental image with the man sitting beside her, but they didn't seem to match.

"When you have an IQ as high as mine, it's hard to fit in. I skipped ahead in school, so I was always around older kids, and they didn't want anything to do with me. Plus I would get lost in my own world and didn't care about anything else."

"What changed?"

He was silent for a moment. "My father left when I was twelve. He always wanted an athletic son—someone he could be proud of. He wanted to go to football games, not science fairs. One day, he just walked out on me and my mom and never came back. I guess I thought if I could be the son he wanted, he would return."

"Did he come back?"

"Nope."

Kaitlyn didn't know what to say. Finally, she said, "I don't think he left because you weren't athletic enough. That doesn't seem to make sense."

"You're right, but I was a kid, I didn't know that at the time. I guess, in a way, I'm glad. Glad he left, glad he didn't come back. It was good for me to get out of my comfort zone. I started running and lifting weights. I joined a couple of clubs in school and learned to be more social. By the time I made it to college, I wasn't such an awkward disaster."

"I don't remember what I was like when I was younger."

Lucas entwined his fingers with hers. "I'm sure you were amazing."

"Quess found a Facebook page that had images of me on it. She said I needed help in the style department. That my clothing was lame, but that doesn't tell much about my personality does it?"

Lucas squeezed her hand. "I think what's important is who you are now. You have a second chance at life. I know it's easy for me to say since I'm not in your shoes, but Kate I'd hate for you to be miserable for the rest of your existence."

Kaitlyn didn't even think about the

consequences of her next question; she didn't consider how awkward it would be for him to answer. "Why did they have to take my memories?"

Lucas stiffened, his face stricken. It was a minute before he gathered his thoughts and was able to answer. "We thought it would be easier for you to adjust to your new life if you couldn't recall your old one."

"I don't even know if I have any family."

"If you knew you had family, would you want to see them?"

Kaitlyn thought it over for a few moments and shook her head. "No. I know that life is over. They think I'm dead. I also understand the reason for the secrecy. I guess I just wish I could remember it."

"I'm sorry, Kate." Lucas tugged her into a bear hug, speaking against her hair. "We were working blind. We had no idea what we were doing. You're the first of your kind."

Kaitlyn pulled away and met his gaze. "Maybe you'll do better with the next *project*."

She caught a flicker of something in his eyes. The facial program scanned images, looking for its equivalent. The answer promptly blinked on her internal screen: Regret, or maybe sadness.

"It would help our next project if we told Harrington and Adams that you still have emotions. That way, we'll know it isn't necessary to erase them for the next…person."

Kaitlyn turned away. "I don't want that. At least, not right now. Don't tell. Please."

"Your secret is safe with me."

The wind blew. Lucas shivered, and Kaitlyn wondered what that felt like. She sat with her back to him, gazing out over the darkening yard. The fence was visible in the distance—the fence that penned her in.

"Lucas, when will I be leaving?" she asked quietly.

"The day after tomorrow you'll meet with the committee. Then they'll negotiate. I'm not sure how long that will take. Could be days, weeks or even months."

"Is there any way out of this?"

"As you know, there are always alternate scenarios. But Harrington is dead-set on releasing you to the government. I can't think of a single reason that would convince him otherwise. Believe me, it's been keeping me up at night trying to come up with something Harrington would go for."

"I could run away."

Lucas turned to face her. "Yes, you could run away, but then what? You would be on your own. What if something happened with your programming? Like the way you shut down the other day. It would be impossible for you to hide in society. The upgrades have helped, but you'd still have trouble blending in for a long period of time with the general populace. Not to mention you have GPS installed. They'll find you."

As much as she hated to admit it, she knew he was right. Perhaps the new life wouldn't be bad. Maybe she would come to enjoy her new existence the way she had the compound. It would certainly be easier to accept the changes if Lucas was there with her.

"Could you come with me? Maybe work for the government and oversee the project?"

Lucas sighed and ran his hand through her hair. "If only it were that easy. But I'm not ready to give up. I'm going to hound Harrington to make sure he insists that we have some oversight of the project. It should be easy enough to convince him that it's needed in order to proceed with stage two."

"More cyborgs?"

"Eventually. It took us a long time to find you, and I don't think it will be any easier to find a new subject. We've been searching all this time with no luck. Not many people offer to donate their body to science within the age requirements and fitness abilities."

"I'm…" Kaitlyn scanned her memory banks, trying to come up with the correct word to fit the situation. "Grateful for the time we were able to have together."

Lucas cupped her face in his hands and

leaned in to kiss her gently. The kiss quickly intensified. When he kissed her, everything else faded away. All she was aware of was his scent, his lips on hers, and how warm his hands felt on her body.

Abruptly, her sensors picked up on another presence. Apparently, he couldn't block out everything.

Kaitlyn's eyes flew open, and she pulled away, jumping up. "Someone is coming."

Lucas looked around and didn't see or hear anything, but he knew better than to question her. He stood up, brushing off his slacks. "We should head back."

"I wish we could stay here forever. Away from everyone."

"Me too," he said softly. He stepped closer and kissed her one last time.

As they were walking back, one of the guards came into view. "There you are. We lost you on the cameras after a while and became concerned. Everything okay?"

Lucas nodded. "We're fine. We were just taking a walk and testing out Katilyn's new upgrades. We must have been in a blind spot."

"There are a couple of those, unfortunately. Perhaps we should have a guard patrolling those areas more often," the guard said, more to himself than to them.

"Not a bad idea." Lucas tried for ambivalence,

but his voice sounded strained to Kaitlyn.

With a quick nod, the guard walked in the opposite direction.

"So much for that hiding spot," Kaitlyn said sadly.

"We'll just have to find another."

Kaitlyn was suddenly flooded with sadness. *Even if it is only for one more day...*

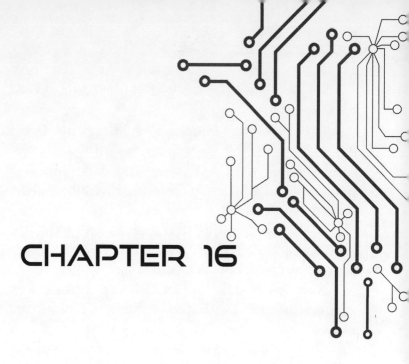

CHAPTER 16

Mr. Harrington strolled into the laboratory on a wave of expensive-smelling cologne. "Who's up for paintball?" he boomed, breaking the silence so abruptly that Professor Adams jumped at his desk. "I need to stretch my legs, and we should try out the new equipment."

Kaitlyn bit the inside of her lip and looked down at her sneakers to keep from smiling. She loved the rare chances she had to roam in the woods, and playing a true sport instead of staged tests. This only happened when the highly competitive Harrington was around.

"I'm game," Lucas said from behind his desk. He snuck a peak at Kate and their eyes met across the room.

"How about you, Adams?" Harrington asked with a smile.

The professor chuckled, holding up both hands. "I think I'll pass this time. My old body can't keep up with you youngsters. Last time we played, I had bruises for a week. I'm sure Quess would be interested."

"Call her. Some of the guards are going to join us as well." Harrington turned to Kaitlyn, sizing her up. "They like a challenge."

Adams picked up the phone to call his granddaughter as Lucas asked, "Teams or individual?"

"Individual," Harrington answered with a wolfish smile.

Lucas groaned. Kaitlyn always won when they played individual.

"Let's get suited up." Harrington rubbed his hands together in front of his face. "Kaitlyn, no body gear for you."

She nodded. They would have the camouflage to help them, and her pale skin would be like a beacon in the sunlight, giving them somewhat of an edge. *Theoretically*, she thought with an inward grin, her hard drive already computing the odds.

Half an hour later, the players gathered in the foyer, and they made their way outside and deep into the property. It was a crisp fall day and the sun shone brightly through the bare tree limbs above them as they came to a stop in the area they used for paintball.

After defining the boundaries, Dr. Harrington laid out some basic ground rules.

"Okay, it's a free-for-all. Everybody against everybody. If you're hit and out, move to this area." He pointed at a spot on the map. "Once there's only one person left, they're the winner. We'll have a three minute 'get in place' period, then we'll start. Any questions?"

Heads shook. A few of the guards had smiles in anticipation of the fun.

Harrington clapped once. "Spread out. Three minutes. Go."

There was a mad scuffle as the guards jostled each other and then ran off into the forest, but Kaitlyn calmly walked into the nearest grove of trees and stopped. Crouching down, she watched the internal clock in her head count down three minutes as she closed her eyes and focused on the sounds around her. Her built-in tactical computer worked through several different strategies based on her knowledge of the area and her assessments on all the various players and what they might do given their backgrounds, physical fitness, injuries, and even attitudes she had observed in the past.

Before the three minutes were up, she had decided on a course of action. Not necessarily the most tactically sound, but given her enhancements, it would be a good test of how much of an advantage she really had. A slow smile spread across her face. She loved the hunt.

Right on the mark, she opened her eyes and took off running at full speed through the shrubs and the trees. She had a mental image of where targets might be, and that image refreshed dozens of times a second as she took in more sights and sounds. They couldn't have made it too far in three minutes.

A sense of calm engulfed her body. She was in her element.

Without breaking stride, she started to engage. One at a time, she took out the enemy.

The targets didn't even hear her coming before they felt the sharp sting of paintballs splatting against them. A couple of times, someone *saw* her before she shot them, but of all the eight other people playing, only one of the guards came remotely close to hitting her, sort of a 'spray and pray' style attack when he thought she would expose herself in a gap between some trees.

After a session lasting only nine minutes, Harrington decided to lay out a handicap for Kaitlyn for the next session.

"Well that was interesting. And painful," Harrington said. "Lets see if we can prolong the next game just a bit. Kaitlyn, I'm going to pair you with Quess. She's your principal who you have to protect. Lucas, you'll be a principal as well, with Tim, Jimmy, and Cal on your team. I'll be the third principal with Craig and Terry on my team.

If you're hit, you're out. If your principal is hit, your whole team is out. Three minutes to get set. Questions?"

Again, no one said anything, and the teams moved away from each other into the woods.

"What are we going to do?" Quess asked eagerly.

"Not get shot." Kate smiled.

Quess nodded, gripping her paintball gun tightly with both hands.

Kaitlyn ran an analysis on her friend, noting the bead of sweat at her hairline and the pinch between her brows. "You're nervous."

Quess laughed. "Don't do that!"

"Don't be nervous." Kaitlyn grinned. "Either way, if we win or lose, this will be fun. Let's go."

"I have to say, it's pretty awesome how badass you are," Quess muttered as they moved forward.

Kaitlyn didn't respond, but at times like this, she almost enjoyed her new body.

With the new team configuration, the second session lasted more than twice as long, twenty-one minutes, but the outcome was the same. Lucas's team lost a member to an early engagement with Mr. Harrington's team before they broke contact and sprinted away, but after that, Kaitlyn made short work of the other two teams.

Instead of running, this time Kaitlyn moved

silently forward through the brush with Quess positioned about one meter to her right rear. Every minute they would stop, crouch, and Kaitlyn would take in the sights, sounds, and smells around her, updating her internal tactical "map" and changing direction or the speed of their movement.

She was crouched at the top of a hill, listening when she heard the crack of a branch in the distance. Kaitlyn motioned for Quess to lay prone behind a tree and cover her. Studying the most likely avenue of approach, Kaitlyn maintained her crouch and waited.

After only a few minutes, she saw the first member of Harrington's team, Terry, cross perpendicular to her position about forty meters away. Not wanting to squander her chance to take out the entire team at once, Kaitlyn waited until she had all three members identified and tracked, then in rapid succession, she shot each one in the chest. Engagement time: three seconds. She heard a few slang words mumbled as they made their way off the playing grounds.

She repeated the same tactic with Lucas's team, again waiting until the three remaining members were in sight. Right before she fired, a brief thought flashed through her mind: *I wonder if Lucas will be upset that I shot him?*

Lucas looked up and grinned shaking his head.

Kaitlyn returned the private smile, before she moved onto the next target.

Once everyone was back at the start point, Harrington wrapped up the game. "While I enjoyed that immensely, it's time I get back to the lab. I don't think I'm alone in not wanting to be shot by Kaitlyn anymore?"

Several of the guards looked over at Kaitlyn, nodding in agreement as they murmured their admiration.

Harrington surprised Kaitlyn by draping his arm around her shoulder. "I couldn't be more proud. You are simply incredible."

She wasn't sure why they were so impressed. She was programmed to be this way.

CHAPTER 17

"Where are we going?" Kaitlyn whispered as they crept past another cluster of brick buildings obscured by darkness.

Quess smiled mysteriously. "You'll see…"

Kaitlyn had never been to this side of the compound and couldn't help but wonder what Quess was up to. The young girl had pulled her from her room after dinner and acted like they were stealth bombers sneaking through the compound as they ducked behind walls as employees passed, unaware.

Tomorrow was the big day. Kaitlyn's 'unveiling,' as Harrington liked to call it. As much as she enjoyed spending time with Quess, she was really hoping to see Lucas alone.

Now, outside in the cold, dark evening, they flitted beneath the orange circles of lamplight, Quess encouraging Kaitlyn to move faster.

"Why are we in such a hurry?" Kaitlyn said with a chuckle.

Quess skidded to a stop, gazing up at a large brick building with no visible windows and ignored the question.

"This way." Quess grabbed her hand and pulled her towards the door.

Kaitlyn did a scan of the outside of the building: All clear. The door screeched against the concrete, and then they were inside.

Inside, it appeared to be a large, dimly lit warehouse. Aisles and aisles of metal shelving were filled with food and other supplies, but a thermal scan proved they were alone.

What in the world is Quess up to now?

They zigzagged through the aisles toward the back of the building where a Jeep was parked at the open loading dock, parked halfway into the building. Lucas jumped out of the vehicle and swung the back door open.

Just the sight of him caused a flush to spread across her face as her body temperature climbed several degrees.

"Get in. We don't have much time."

Without hesitation, Kaitlyn climbed into the back of the Jeep. Lucas covered her body with a soft blanket. Kate lifted the blanket and peered out.

"What about Quess?"

Quess looked down into the back of the jeep. "I'm just an accomplice this time. Stay safe, Kaitlyn."

Kate nodded and pulled the blanket back over her head.

"Be still. We just have to make it through the guard gate. If we get caught let me take the blame, don't harm the guard." The back door clicked into place and moments later, the engine came to life and they rolled slowly down the road. Kaitlyn's senses were on high alert, listening for any sign of danger.

Seven minutes later, the Jeep stopped. She could hear the window roll down. "Hey, Matt. Long day?"

"The usual. We've been doing random checks of vehicles. Lucky you, you've been flagged. Step out for a minute, will you Lucas?"

"Since when?" Lucas asked.

"Started this morning. Hop out, will you?

""Look, it's been a long day, man. I just want to get home," Lucas said smoothly.

Kaitlyn's breathing remained steady, and her mind raced to figure out the best course of action.

"Out of the car, Lucas."

The door opened, and there was a thump as Lucas dropped to the ground. "Ridiculous," he muttered under his breath.

"Pop the hood," the guard barked, all business.

Kaitlyn heard the thump as the hood opened, and a moment later, Lucas muttered, "Satisfied?"

Kaitlyn tensed, expecting the guard to demand that Lucas open the back door. She had been warned not to harm the guard, so her computer kicked into gear, searching for an alternative.

"Not yet." The hood slammed shut. "Open the back, and then I'll do a quick sweep underneath."

Kaitlyn listened as their foot steps echoing on the concrete. The door swung open. Stillness settled over her. Through the blanket, she saw a flashlight swoop over her.

"How long are they going to do this nonsense?" Lucas asked, distracting the guard.

"Who knows. They said it would be random." The door slammed shut.

"Can I go now?" Lucas asked.

"Yeah, man. See you tomorrow. Just following orders."

"I hear you. It's just annoying. I've been here twelve hours and ready to call it a night." Lucas shut his door and started the engine.

"Take it easy," the guard yelled as the Jeep rolled forward.

Close call. Kaitlyn let out the breath she didn't realize she'd been holding. She was jostled when they rolled over a speed bump. Lucas had put himself at risk for her. What did this mean? Was she really escaping? Her body revved up at the prospect.

They drove for a short while before Kaitlyn felt the vehicle's gears shift and begin to slow. They came to a stop, and the back door swung open.

Kaitlyn launched herself at Lucas, her arms wrapping around his neck. "I can't believe you got me off the compound."

His face seemed paler than usual. "We got lucky. Of all the days to do a stupid vehicle check. If it had been anyone other than me, he would have gone over the Jeep with a fine-toothed comb." He tucked a strand of her hair behind her ear.

"What now? Where are we going to go?"

Lucas's face fell, and his shoulders slumped. "It's not like that, Kate. We're not leaving forever. They'd hunt us down, and I'd go to prison, and then they would probably shut down your system."

"Oh." Kaitlyn stepped away from him, suddenly sad. This wasn't an escape; she would be going back to the compound. She would be sold as a top secret super soldier. She focused on the fact that she was alone with Lucas, and that would have to be enough for now. And he thought she was worth losing his job over. That alone spoke volumes.

"Why did you do this? You could lose your job or worse."

"I wanted to spend some time alone with you. Tomorrow, you might be leaving for good." He leaned down and pressed his lips to hers. Reluctantly, he pulled away. "You're worth the risk."

"Won't they realize we're off the property?"

"We'll only have a couple of hours. If anyone checks the tapes, they'll see you leave with Quess, and they'll expect you've been with her the whole time. I also put a glitch in your GPS to make it appear as if you haven't left."

Kaitlyn thought about this information. She could knock Lucas out and take off, leaving the compound for good. But as soon as he put the GPS back online they would be able to find her. Lucas would lose his job, and potentially worse.

She stood on her tiptoes and kissed his warm lips once more. "Thank you. Where are we going?"

"We can't go too far away, I'm afraid."

"I don't care, as long as I'm with you."

Lucas grabbed her hand and led her over to the passenger side. She slid into the front seat. Once Lucas was in the driver side, he placed his hand on Kaitlyn's lap. His warm hand against her cool skin sent shivers through her. Being around him made her feel like a woman, not a thing. Her body responded to his touch in ways that sent her mind spinning. She never wanted to leave his side.

They drove five miles, then Lucas flicked on his blinker and turned down a narrow, unpaved side road. The area was remote—not a house in sight. The Jeep was surrounded on all sides by towering trees. It seemed like all she saw was trees.

"I come here sometimes," he said, "to think."

Kaitlyn tilted her head to the side. "You have a place you go to think?" she asked, bewildered.

Lucas squeezed her hand. "It's relaxing. You'll see."

He continued driving. The road got narrower and steeper. The sun had set long ago, and the sky was pitch dark this deep in the woods. Finally, Lucas pulled the Jeep to a halt at the top of what appeared to be a ledge. He left the lights on and hurried around to open her door, but Kaitlyn had already climbed out.

"One minute. I have to grab something from the back."

He returned with the blanket in his arms. Anticipation coursed through Kaitlyn's body.

"I'm sorry I can't take you out on a proper date, but time is limited and the compound is away from civilization. It takes ages to anywhere. I was going to pack a picnic, but I remembered you don't need to eat. So I thought we could just look at the stars, and get to know each other better."

"Ages? It can't really be that far for civilization?"

Lucas laughed. "Slight exaggeration on my part."

Kaitlyn glanced up at the sky and saw white sparkles in the darkness. Crickets chirped in the distance. She could hear the steady rush of water somewhere close by. Her mind flashed with potential rivers, narrowing down the location.

Lucas spread the blanket on the ground.

Hesitantly, Kaitlyn closed the distance between them. Lucas's hands slid down her arms and pulled her close, her body molding against his as if they were made for each other. Kaitlyn slid her hand under his shirt and spread her fingers across his back. Heat radiated off him, and his breathing increased. She smiled to herself, knowing she had caused the reaction. His lips brushed hers lightly, and an urgency spread through her body. She couldn't get close enough.

Breaking free from the kiss, Kaitlyn pulled him down onto the blanket. Lucas kissed her again, their legs tangled together. He broke the kiss, rolling to the side so they were facing each other. His hand gently trailed down her face, her arm, and her thigh. Her body felt like it was on fire.

Kaitlyn pushed up his shirt and ran her

hands over his chest. It was hard and warm. She couldn't believe this was happening. It was like a dream come true. His lips trailed down her neck, causing her to gasp with pleasure. How could he have such an effect on her? It was mind-boggling. She closed her eyes and let the feeling take over.

His heart pounded, and it was music to her ears. Kaitlyn pulled away and lifted off her shirt, giving only a passing worry to the teal plastic on her skin. Lucas groaned, his heated eyes racing over her chest. Kate fumbled with the button on his pants, and Lucas grabbed her hand.

"Kate, are you sure?"

Her eyes widened in surprise. "What do you mean? Of course I'm sure. This is what men and women do. Just like in the movies."

Lucas sat up abruptly and yanked his shirt down. "Kate, this isn't right. I shouldn't have let it get this far."

"I don't understand."

"I'm taking advantage of you. You don't even comprehend what's going on. What a relationship entails. Hell, we don't even know if you're a virgin."

Kaitlyn reached for her shirt and spread it over her chest. "You don't want to have sex with me?"

"Not like this." He rubbed his hands across his face. "It's not fair to you. That's not what I brought you here for."

"It's not?"

"No, I just wanted to spend time with you."

"Oh." Kaitlyn tried to process that thought, and her processor began to argue the point. "They always have sex in the movies. When I saw the blanket…"

"I care more about you than a roll in the hay."

Kaitlyn looked around. "Hay? I see nothing but grass."

"That's what I mean, Kate. Things are still confusing to you. Come sit by me."

Kate scooted over and Lucas put his arm around her, then pulled it away. "Please put your shirt back on. This is hard enough as it is."

Kaitlyn tugged her shirt back over her head. "Better?"

Lucas didn't reply. Instead, he laid on his back and motioned for her to curl against him. When they were settled, he pointed up at the stars. "Can you pick out Orion?"

Kaitlyn concentrated on the stars and pointed off to the left. "It's right there. It looks like an hourglass. Did you know that in the middle-east, Orion is known as *Al-Jabbar*, 'the giant'?"

Lucas shook his head. "I only know it as The Hunter, from Greek mythology."

They were silent for a long moment, snuggled against each other on the blanket. Kaitlyn stared up at the vast expanse of star-dotted sky above them, acutely aware of his presence beside her.

He spoke up, his arm squeezing her shoulders. "I love sitting under the stars. It seems to put everything else in perspective. We're just a tiny blip in the universe."

"I can see why you like it here," Kaitlyn said softly and laid her head against his shoulder. "Thank you for showing me where you come to think. Do you ever think about me here?"

Lucas nodded, a movement she could feel above her own head. "All the time. I've wrestled with my feelings about you for a long time."

Over an hour passed of them sitting in peaceful silence. Once in a while, Lucas would point out another constellation, and Kate would report random facts that coincided with that particular grouping of stars. They would laugh at her seemingly endless well of knowledge.

"We should probably head back. The guards have changed shifts. I should be able to get you back without any trouble."

"I wish I could stay here forever," Kaitlyn said wistfully.

"We'll see what happens tomorrow. Hopefully, you won't have to leave right away. I think I've finally convinced Harrington to make a condition of the sale that I'm able to watch over you."

"Really?" Kaitlyn bit her bottom lip. If she could still see Lucas, she could handle anything.

"Really. I know it's hard for you to believe,

but he really doesn't want to give you up. He's very invested in this project. Now let's get you back before we get Quess in trouble."

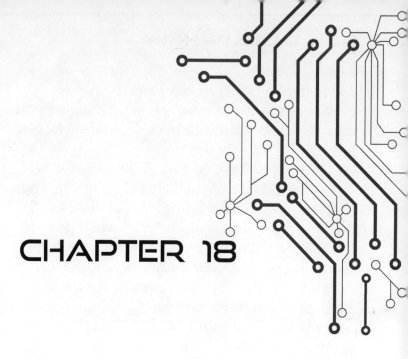

CHAPTER 18

Kaitlyn sat in the empty, sterile room for two hours, thirteen minutes, and six seconds before she heard familiar footsteps echoing off the tiles down the hall. Usually, the sound caused her heart rate to increase, but today it filled her with dread.

Shoulders slumped, Lucas stepped into the lab. His face looked strained. His hair was disheveled like he just rolled out of bed. "Kaitlyn. It's time."

"I don't want to go," she whispered. "Can't I stay here?"

"I'm sorry, Kate." His eyes were full of regret. "It's way past that point. I will do everything I can to make sure I can stay a part of the program.

That's the best we have right now."

She wanted to argue; to start listing tactical alternatives to their situation. Instead, her voice hardened. "Let's get this over with."

"Kate, you have to believe me. I really wish things could be different." He held open the door for her, and she brushed past him. Even now, his touch sent an electrical charge down her spine. It's not fair, Kaitlyn thought, surprised at how much emotion welled up inside of her.

In the hallway outside, Harrington stood as rigid as a board waiting for them. Kaitlyn had never before seen him so tense. She wondered if he overheard their conversation, but that was impossible, he was too far away. Humans' hearing wasn't that effective.

"Just be yourself, Kaitlyn, and everything will go fine," he said soothingly like he was talking to a child.

Be myself? She wanted to laugh. She didn't even know what that meant thanks to him. She had no idea who or what she was other than what he had made her.

Despite a desire to punch him, she nodded like the obedient robot she was. She glanced at the doorway and debated making a run for it. She could probably evade the guards since she knew all of their locations, but the fact was that with a click of a few computer keys they could shut her down. Her life was not in her control. The thought angered her, but her feet moved forward even though she wanted to stay rooted to the ground or bolt in the other direction.

The walk down the long corridor felt like she was walking to her demise. Every step forward made her want to turn and run as fast as she could, to get as far away as she could. They left the building and crossed the campus. The sun was shining, the smell of fresh cut grass filled the air and a blue jay chirped as staff members went about their business. Life as usual, she thought bitterly. Meanwhile, her life was about to be uprooted once again.

All Kaitlyn could think about was that she may have been walking away from the IFICS lab for the last time. The thought filled her with an unbearable sadness. Even though the compound was sterile and cold, it had become her home. And the outside, whatever was out there, was scary and unknown. She glanced over at Lucas and her throat tightened.

Maybe human feelings weren't all they were cracked up to be. She almost wished there was a 'turn off emotions' switch.

Harrington led them to a building ten minutes' walk from the lab—yet another section of the massive compound Kaitlyn had never stepped foot in. They had kept her so isolated during her time at the facility. Now it was too late; she would never have the chance to explore the whole compound.

She briefly wondered if she would have more or less freedom once she was sold. Probably less.

When they entered the unfamiliar building, Kaitlyn glanced around, taking in the new surroundings. Unlike the stark, sterile lab, there wasn't a white wall to be seen. Lots of browns, greens, and maroon. Abstract paintings hung strategically on the walls, and a large, fanciful vase of wildflowers sat on the reception table in front of the main doors. As they approached, a curvy blonde woman rose from behind the reception desk and smiled. "Good morning. They are waiting inside."

"Thanks, Gracie."

Harrington led the way and continued through a set of massive wooden double doors and into a large conference room. There were several men and women sitting behind a long table, backs straight and all eyes solely on Kaitlyn as she entered. Many were dressed in military uniforms. Kaitlyn's computer scanned each for identification: High-ranking officials from three different branches. Army, Navy and Air Force. 'Caution' flashed on her internal screen. Thanks computers, she thought, slightly annoyed. *I'm well aware the situation is problematic.*

She felt oddly detached from herself. She had to accept her new fate. Whatever was in store for her, she could handle. She would handle. After all, she had been programmed and prepared extensively for this day. Her eyes strayed to Lucas and she knew she was only trying to fool herself. She really didn't want to leave. His eyes met hers and her heart sank.

Harrington approached the head of the table and Kaitlyn stood off to the side with Lucas to the left of her. She felt calmer by his presence. She was surprised to see that Professor Adams was not in the room.

Mr. Harrington took to the podium. "Ladies and Gentlemen, it is with great pride that I would like to introduce to you, Kaitlyn. The first true cyborg of our time. Her skills surpass even the most seasoned solider, and with more training, she will only get better. Human nature and technology have collided, and as you can see, the outcome is spectacular. Where others have failed, we have surpassed even our own highest expectations."

A murmur of approval went around the table. "Kaitlyn, come up here."

Kaitlyn moved without thinking and made her way to Harrington's side. Everyone was staring at her, looking her up and down from head to toe. Even though she was used to being on display, for some reason the people that were looking at her now made her skin crawl.

An old man with four stars on his collar, and a scowl on his face spoke from the middle of the table. He had an arrow head patch on his right sleeve, which her scan identified as JSOC. She guessed a former Delta Force commander. "Forgive me for not taking your word, Harrington. Are we going to see her in action?"

"Of course. We've put together a short film for you."

With the click of a button on the podium, the lights dimmed and a screen scrolled down on the right wall. Curious, Kaitlyn turned to watch along with her prospective owners.

The film started out in the combat room. Kaitlyn easily flipped Jeff over her shoulder, slamming him to the ground. At six-foot-two, he had been six inches taller than her and outweighed her by almost one-hundred pounds. The man struggled to get back to his feet, and with one swift kick, Kaitlyn swiped his knee cap, bringing him to his knees. The man howled in pain and swung blindly, but Kaitlyn easily blocked the blow. Like an animal, Kaitlyn circled her prey. In the blink of an eye, her arms were wrapped around his neck, and he went slack. Unconscious.

Live Fire flashed across the screen, and then there was Kaitlyn, sprinting through the woods, weaponless. Suddenly, she dropped flat to the ground as a bullet whizzed past. She crawled into the brush. Within seconds, she located the target, waited until they were on top of her, sprung to her feet, and engaged. In the blink of an eye she had the shooter's gun in her own hands and pressed against his temple before he knew what happened. The man smirked and raised his hands. Kaitlyn lowered the gun.

It cut to Kaitlyn at the shooting range. Fifty-five meters flashed across the screen. Kaitlyn held a pistol and fired off shots, first using only her right hand, and then the left. The target came forward and showed a small, tight circle on the forehead of the silhouette.

Someone muttered, "Impossible." Several heads turned her way. She was surprised to feel a flush of pleasure from their awe.

There were a few more brief scenes showcasing her skills, and then the room went dark briefly before the lights flashed back on.

Everyone stared at Kaitlyn with renewed interest. Even the stoic older gentleman in the middle sat up in his seat and seemed impressed.

"How do we know this is not doctored?" a stern-faced brunette woman asked. Her hair was pulled up so tightly in a bun her eyes were slanted back. Kaitlyn wondered if it gave her a headache. She wasn't in uniform so Kaitlyn had no idea who she was representing.

"You're welcome to watch her in the field. I just wanted to give you a quick glimpse into her potential. Ladies and gentlemen, what we have seen here only scratches the surface. She can sense targets before they even become a threat. Her body temperature controls itself in any environment. The list goes on and on. I don't want to give away all her secrets until we know for sure there is interest."

A woman from the end of the table spoke up. "Oh, there's interest all right. What's the downside?" Kaitlyn blinked at the questions and waited for his reaction. She had never thought of the downsides herself. Surely, there must be some.

Harrington paced before them for a moment. "Really, the only downside is perception. Society is not ready for something of this magnitude. She would have to be kept top secret."

"Well, that's easy enough," the woman replied. "Who would want to risk such a gold mine in the public eye anyway? We would keep her locked away until needed."

Kaitlyn tensed up. So she had her answer: yet again she would be locked away. Only this time, there would be no Lucas or Quess.

"So." Harrington clapped his hands together, rubbing them. "Where should we start the bidding?"

"Not so fast." Said the surly man in the middle of the table. Kaitlyn's scan calculated him to be the most dangerous of the crew despite his age. A person doesn't get to his level with out being a threat. "A video might be good enough to catch our attention, but we need to see her in a real environment before we talk money."

"Very well. You can use my compound to set up any scenarios you wish. I assure you that she will pass with flying colors."

A tall, slim man in his mid-forties stood up. He was wearing an Air Force uniform, and the name on his tag said Fenderson. "I would like to speak to the subject."

Harrington nodded to Kaitlyn, and she stepped forward.

The man directed his question to her. "What can you tell us about yourself?"

"My name is Kaitlyn. I am programmed to be efficient and deadly. I follow orders without hesitation." She stood with her hands to her sides, motionless, and spoke in a monotone voice.

Nods of approval went around the room. Like Harrington they also wanted a mindless robot. The thought caused her to clench her hands into fist.

Another woman, with short grey hair, spoke. "I think she would have a hard time blending in. She sounds like a robot. With her looks she will draw a lot of attention. Some missions might require she interact in public, even if on a limited basis."

"We've been working on that. We have installed a slang chip and facial recognition program so she can mimic emotions when needed. Which brings up another issue. If you are interested, we would like our main programmer to stay involved." He nodded towards Lucas.

"He's not much more than a boy. We have our own people," one of the men said curtly.

The old man nodded. "I'm afraid the only way we could agree to this project is if we have complete control. Once she left this compound, everything would be in the black. Top secret, even to you. If you and your team were involved there would be an increased risk."

"Not acceptable," Harrington said firmly. "My team is to remain with Kaitlyn or there will be no negotiations."

"Do you really want to be the ones to take responsibility if something went wrong?" another man asked. "If the subject is handed over to the government, you will not be responsible for any of the backlash. What you've done in creating your cyborg is illegal. By handing her over to us, you would be free and clear of any legal recriminations were knowledge of her existence to hit the media."

"I don't give a shit about backlash," Harrington said. "She was my vision. And pardon me for not quite taking your word. The government has been known to throw people under the bus when it suits their needs."

"Then you would be seeking another buyer." The older man in the middle folded his hands calmly in front of him on the table. Outwardly he appeared calm, but his heart rate had increased substantially. Kaitlyn knew he was bluffing. But he seemed to be in charge of the show. Everyone else remained quiet.

The usually calm Harrington's jaw was clenched, and a flush rose to his face. "Fine. I believe this meeting has reached its end. When you are ready to be sensible, you know how to reach me. I don't think I have to remind you there are other potential buyers. Out of loyalty to my country I gave you first chance." He turned on his heel and strode from the room. Kaitlyn and Lucas followed close behind.

Harrington slammed the door open with a thud.

"Those arrogant jackasses. She is mine! They cannot expect me to hand over something I have put my heart and soul into and just walk away."

"I thought you expected this." Lucas raised an eyebrow.

"I know, but when we are so close to handing her over, I can't do it. I need time to think. Make sure those fools make it off the compound."

For the first time, hope rose in Kaitlyn's chest. Maybe Harrington would find a way to keep control. Which meant she could keep Lucas.

"Why didn't the others bid?" Kaitlyn asked confused.

"It wasn't a bidding war. All the branches work together for SOCOM, so it would have been a joint project. Harrington never planned on giving anyone a chance at you. He just wanted them to offer the maximum amount of money. Harrington is a lot of things, but he's not a traitor to his country."

Kaitlyn let the info sink in. If the government officials didn't change their minds, what would become of her?

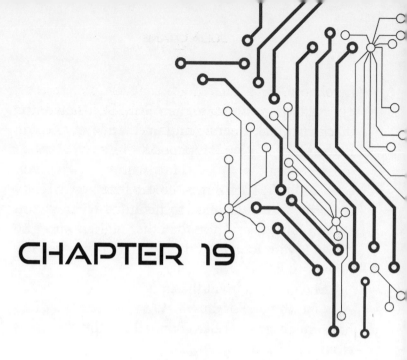

CHAPTER 19

Kaitlyn sat on her bed with her arms wrapped around her legs, lost in thought. She'd been in the same position for over an hour—since she returned from the meeting—but had barely noticed the passage of time.

Back and forth emotions pulled her in different directions. Could Harrington convince the buyer to allow Lucas to be a part of the package? If not, she'd be starting a new life all over again. Her sensors picked up on Lucas down the hall, moving quickly in her direction, but she was too worried to care. Soon, she could be gone. He was probably coming to take her away now.

Lucas rushed into her room without bothering to knock. "We have to get you out of here, now."

Kaitlyn jumped to her feet. She noted the black rucksack in one hand and a pile of clothing in the other. "What happened?"

"Harrington caved. He's willing to give you over as long as he gets credit for you. I really thought he would stick to his guns on this. You should have heard him the other night. I know he doesn't want to give you up, but he thinks it's the only option."

She glanced up at the camera.

"Disabled. For now. Hurry, Kate. We don't have much time." Lucas handed her the change of clothing. "Put these on."

"Where will I go?" she asked, clutching the all-black clothing to her chest as she stared at him.

"As far away from this place as possible. I have money saved up. You can start over."

"Start over? Without you?" It felt like someone was pressing on her chest and she couldn't breathe.

"It's for the best. They'll turn you into a killer, Kate. I can't stand the thought of that. I'm not going to let it happen."

Kaitlyn dropped the pile of clothes on her bed. She stepped forward, cupping his face in her hands. His eyes were wild. "I don't want to leave you."

She rose on her tiptoes to kiss him in an attempt to calm him. And for a moment, his heart rate slowed. The rucksack he held hit the floor with a thud, and he pressed his body against hers. As the kiss deepened, he grasped her by both arms and pushed her away.

"Kate, don't you get it? Either way, you leave me. They will never allow us to be together. They want someone with no ties, no emotions. Now that I know you can feel, I can't allow them to do this to you. I don't care if I lose my job or get sent to jail." His gaze swept across her face as if he was drinking in the sight of her and he plunged his hands into her hair. "I can't let them have you."

"Where would I go? I don't exactly blend in," Kaitlyn murmured, her hands resting on his chest, her mind filtering through all the information.

"You can blend in, Kate. You just have to wear long clothing to cover what we've done to you. Don't get in long conversations with people. Keep to yourself."

"It won't work, and you know it," Kaitlyn said. "You're shaking, and that's why." She covered his hands with her own. "There is no way out of this for me. I should just go, Lucas. It's not worth you getting in trouble. It's too big of a risk."

"It's my risk to take. You have to try. Please, Kate."

She bit her lip, scanning her mind for options. "Do you have a plan?"

"Of course. But, Kate… I can't know where you are. If I know, I will look for you. I can't lead them to you. They'll watch me, they'll watch all of us once you escape."

Escape. The word sounded so foreign to her. She reluctantly stepped away from his warm embrace and tugged off the clothes she wore. She could feel Lucas's eyes on her as she dressed in the black pants and pulled the long sleeved black shirt over her head. "What about the GPS?"

"I'm going to fry it. They won't be able to track you. As long as you stay out of the limelight."

"Limelight?" Kaitlyn frowned.

Lucas smiled sadly. "Just don't get caught."

He pulled her close and kissed her deeply, as if he only had a moment left to live. It literally took her breath away.

"I still don't know how you do that to me," she said against his lips, stealing one more kiss.

He brushed a strand of her hair out of her face. "Whatever you feel is magnified by a thousand for me. God, I'm going to miss you." His voice was hoarse.

Kaitlyn opened her mouth to argue such a thing was not statistically possible, but something overrode the reaction. She realized without having to be told that he was just being sweet. But was it her computer that recognized the sentiment, or the real Kate?

"Kate, I'm going to do something I should have done a long time ago. I hope you can forgive me for all I've taken from you."

"Lucas don't say that, none of this is your fault. You were just a pawn in Harrington's game."

"Shh." He pressed his finger to her lips. "Turn around."

"What are you going to do?"

"I'm giving you your past back. Memories of your old life."

Kaitlyn's breathing hitched and she paused in the act of turning to look at him seriously. "My real life? Human life?"

Lucas nodded. "I programmed it so that your memories won't hit you for thirty minutes. That should give you more than enough time to get off the compound."

"But how? I thought they were gone…"

He closed his eyes, pained. "Not gone, Kate. Saved to a hard drive and taken away from you."

"They saved my memories?"

Opening his eyes, he said, "No. I did."

Kaitlyn couldn't stop her jaw from dropping. "Do they know?"

He shook his head.

"Why would you save them?"

"Because I cared about the girl you were before you came to us." Before she could ask another question, Lucas went on. "I can't take you through this time. I need an alibi once they realize you've escaped. It will give you more time. I'll have to sound the alarm when Harrington sends me to pick you up, and I find the room empty."

Pivoting on the balls of her feet, she threw her arms around his neck, pulling him in for one last kiss. The thought of never tasting his lips on hers again made her feel hollow. "Thank you." A small part of her was annoyed that he had her memories the whole time, but she pushed the thought aside. He was risking so much for her.

Once they broke away, Lucas looked at her sadly. She wondered if his heart was hurting as much as hers. "Let me implant the chip to override the commands. I wish I had known you then, Kaitlyn."

Kaitlyn hesitated, and then slowly, she turned around. He pulled down her shirt and kissed her neck. There was an audible click and she felt a pinch as something was inserted into her mainframe.

"Okay, it's done."

She turned to face him, and he handed her an iPhone. Kaitlyn had never seen one before, but it would be easy enough to figure out.

"There are maps on here and access to information. The phone is not traceable. If you need information, double click on the round button and speak into the phone, asking it what you need."

Kaitlyn looked at him like he was crazy. "You want me to talk into the device, and it will answer me?"

"I know it sounds silly, but it really works."

"Where am I going to go?"

"I-I don't know. Just trust your instincts. Remember, try not to draw attention to yourself. Harrington will not stop looking for you."

"I don't want to say goodbye."

"It's the only way." He whispered. "Don't underestimate the guards, Kate, they know what they're doing."

She shot him a look. "I'll be fine. I'm quite efficient, thanks to IFICS."

Lucas looked down at the floor. A flush of red covered his cheeks. "I'll still worry about you. Every day."

Kaitlyn reached for his hand and entwined his fingers in hers. His hand was large and warm in her own; it felt so natural. How could she walk away from him? And Quess?

"Quess!" she blurted out.

"I'll tell her you're safe, but you have to go. Now." Lucas picked up the rucksack and handed it to her. "Don't kill anyone getting out. The guards are just doing their job. They all respect you. I think some have even grown to like you."

"No collateral damage. I'll get out without loss of life." She nodded and slung the bag over her shoulders.

Lucas peeked out the door first and motioned for her to follow. They hurried down the empty hallway. At the back door, Lucas came to an abrupt stop. "I have to go back to the lab so I'm seen."

"I'll never be able to repay you for giving me my freedom back. I will find you again," Kaitlyn told him, her heart pounding.

Lucas's eyes glistened under the fluorescent lights. "Goodbye, Kate. I'll never forget you."

Pushing the metal door open, Lucas hurried to the right, and Kaitlyn silently took off to the left, blending into the night. Her night vision kicked in, and her eyes adjusted quickly to the darkness. She had to admit the technology came in handy. At first, it had taken her a bit to get used to, but now it felt no different than her day sight. It was an advantage the guards did not have, at least not automatically like she did. They would have to go to the supply closet and pick up night vision goggles, buying her more time.

Kaitlyn knew the location of all the guards, and she also knew that at any minute they would be alerted that she had escaped. She had to act fast.

She flitted across the campus, aiming for the far reaches of the compound. It only took five minutes before she heard crashing in the bushes behind her. The erratic bouncing of flashlight beams danced around her, followed by excited yelling. Lucas must have sounded the alarm.

A bullet whizzed past her ear. She heard it thump as it hit the grass. They'd spotted her! It took all of her self-control not to turn around and break the guard's neck. Lucas had told her no death. She ran in a zigzag pattern—typical of her training. It was hard to hit a moving target. Let alone at her speed.

Vectoring in through her location sensors, Kaitlyn found the nearest wall almost four hundred meters away. So close. She increased her speed, legs and arms pumping, breaths equal and strong. Just a little further, and she would be free.

Don't think. Just move. Let your body do what it was made to do.

The high fence loomed before her. Skidding to a stop, she tossed her bag over. One quick glance behind her, and she scaled the fence. Once she was close to the barbwire she jumped over, her arms flailing as she fell towards the ground. She hit the ground, bending her knees and tucking in her elbows to absorb the impact.

With one last glance behind her, Kaitlyn shrugged her rucksack on. Her heart constricted and an aching pain filled her chest. *So that was what pain felt like*, she thought sadly.

Move, Kaitlyn scolded herself and took off in a full sprint, disappearing into the night as if she'd never existed.

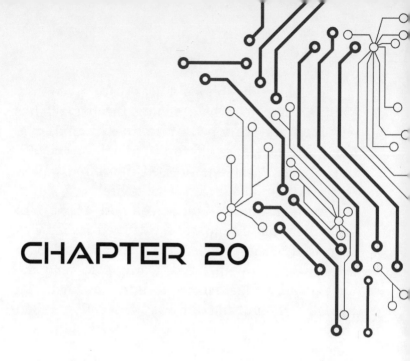

CHAPTER 20

Kaitlyn crashed through the woods, the cracking branches beneath her feet filling the dark silence. The green-tinted night forest spread around her as far as she could see. She had been on the run for thirteen minutes and eleven seconds. Scanning the forest she could see the body heat of several startled animals. There wasn't a human form in sight. If they were chasing her, they weren't close — at least, not yet.

Faster.

She had to get out of the woods and into civilization; a town. There had to be a town near here, somewhere. They would be combing the woods for her for days, but she didn't plan on being there that long.

Recalling the phone Lucas had given her, Kaitlyn came to a halt, swung the bag off her shoulder and dropped it to the ground. She unzipped the side pocket and slid out the smooth, thin phone. When she pressed the round button on the bottom, the screen came to life.

A small square on the screen said 'Maps.' Not knowing what else to do, she tapped it. She was surprised when it opened to a map. She had spent extensive time with Frank learning to read the terrain and navigate maps. It didn't take her long to realize the pulsing dot was her location. When she moved forward, the dot moved with her. Genius.

There was a major highway approximately fifteen miles due north. She stuffed the phone back in the bag and took off in that direction. The undergrowth was getting thicker, and the hills steeper. Reaching up, she grasped hold of a branch to help pull her forward, and then another until she made it to the top. She broke free of the thick shrubs and trees and found herself standing on the edge of a cliff over a stream.

A wave of dizziness washed over her, and she stumbled back, losing her footing. Had they caused her to malfunction remotely? Closing her eyes, she tried to steady herself, to wait for the dizziness to pass.

But instead, like a tidal wave, her memories came crashing back.

It was too much. She wanted to grab the sides of her head and scream, but as images flashed through her mind and emotions spun her around, she breathed deeply and pulled herself back up the slope. She had to keep moving.

Memories of a young girl streamed through her mind. A young, dark-haired girl stood outside in a raincoat and yellow boots waiting for the bus. She turned and smiled at a woman with dark hair, pale skin, and bright blue eyes. It hit Kaitlyn that the woman was probably her mother and the girl Kaitlyn herself. The next flash was her, slightly older, sitting cross-legged under a Christmas tree. A tall slim man with curly blond hair and grey eyes handed her a wrapped box. The girl squealed when she opened up the box and found ice skates. She threw her arms around the man. "Daddy!"

Daddy. The man was her father. He was wearing a red sweater with a snow man on it. His jaw was chiseled and his eyes were the same color as her own.

Keep moving. The influx of memories weakened her. She wanted to drop to the ground, curl into a ball, and wait for it to stop, but her pursuers could be gaining on her. Lucas had given her a chance, and she wasn't going to let him down.

She seemed happy as a child. She laughed and smiled a lot. Athletic; she raced horses, played soccer, practiced karate, surfed, and later, rock climbed.

Kaitlyn ran faster in the shadows of the trees, pushing herself. Keep moving.

And then she was a teenager. School and parties. Boyfriends, dances, and kisses. She gasped when she saw Evan for the first time. His blond hair was shorter, but his green eyes sparkled just like in her dreams. They walked arm in arm through a park, so natural and happy together. He turned and kissed her. Kaitlyn couldn't help but wonder if his kisses made her feel the way Lucas's had.

She almost tripped over a large root when the next image flashed in front of her vision. Okay, so she definitely wasn't a virgin. One mystery solved, as Quess would say. Just seeing the images of her and Evan naked and entwined together on a twin bed made her temperature start to climb, but her sensors quickly regulated her body.

More memories crashed through, like watching home movies. Kaitlyn's breath caught in her throat when the memories started to dim and she was walking by herself. She finally understood the meaning of hairs standing up on the back of one's neck. She tensed, and came to an abrupt stop.

She was about to see something really bad, she could feel it. It was as if she were back in her old body and feeling what she had felt at the time.

In her mind, she watched herself cross Washington Blvd, the main street of her town. She'd done it a thousand times over her lifetime. She paused at the center line, waiting for a car to pass. A truck: Mr. Freeman from the bakery smiled and waved from the drivers seat. She hurried across the street and turned down Lance Drive, a side street that would get her home faster. It was a moonless night, and the streetlights gave off an eerie glow. That's when she heard it: a woman screaming, begging for someone to stop.

In her memory, Kaitlyn froze, then jumped to action. Whipping out a cell phone, she dialed nine-one-one and in a hushed voice told the operator a woman was being attacked. She gave the street, and clicked off the line. Kaitlyn ran up the hill in the direction of the screams which had softened into muffled whimpers.

She spun around, searching. It took her a few moments to realize the sounds were coming from behind a large dumpster. Kaitlyn gasped when she saw a man on top of a woman, her clothes were ripped and face bloody. The man was too intent on the woman to notice Kaitlyn approaching.

She glanced around, searching for something to use as a weapon. A metal pole was sticking out of the dumpster, so she pulled it out, trying to be quiet. Kaitlyn grasped the pole like a baseball bat and swung as hard as she could at the man's back.

"What the hell?" he screamed slumped forward grabbing his back.

"Help me," the woman said, mascara running down her cheeks. "Please."

"Get off her, you asshole." Kaitlyn's hands shook as she held the metal weapon.

The guy ignored her and kept slamming himself into the defenseless woman as if having Kaitlyn watching turned him on even more.

"Get off her!" She drew back again and smashed him on the head.

That caught his attention. He jerked up, stumbling away from the prone woman. "Bitch." Blood trickled down the side of his face. He pulled his jeans up, but left himself hanging out.

Kaitlyn spared a look at the woman; she was frozen in fear.

The man turned and faced Kaitlyn, completely exposing himself. He grabbed himself, and yelled, "You want some of this?"

Kaitlyn refused to look down. She swung, but the man blocked it and grabbed the pole from her. Kaitlyn took off in a sprint, but he was faster.

He tackled her to the ground and pushed his pants down. His naked body pressed to hers. Her face was shoved into the pavement. "You like it rough? I'll give you rough."

He roughly rolled her around and climbed on top of her.

"No!" Kaitlyn screamed, shoving a hand in his face.

He grabbed her arms and pinned her down, then punched her in the face. "Not so tough now, are you?"

He paused as sirens wailed outside the alley.

"I called the cops, jackass," Kaitlyn spat.

He jumped to his feet, pulled up his jeans and kicked her several times in the side. Searing pain shot through Kaitlyn, sending black spots across her vision. He jerked her to her feet, and she lashed out, scratching his face.

The man howled. "You stupid bitch!"

He shoved her hard, throwing her to the ground. Her head slammed against the sidewalk. Everything started to fade, and the last thing she saw was a bright white light.

The next thing in Kaitlyn's memories was her eyes fluttering open and seeing Lucas's exhausted eyes staring at her by her hospital bed.

So that was how she had died.

"She's awake!" he yelled.

Nurses and doctors. Then several flashes of Lucas reading to her, helping her walk, and brushing her hair. He really was with her the whole time...

Kaitlyn shook her head as the memories came to an end, and she could hear movement. She didn't know how long she'd been stopped, but at least she was hidden in the shadows.

Shaken to the core by the return of her memories, she shook her head, trying to regain momentum. She needed to keep moving or they would close in on her soon.

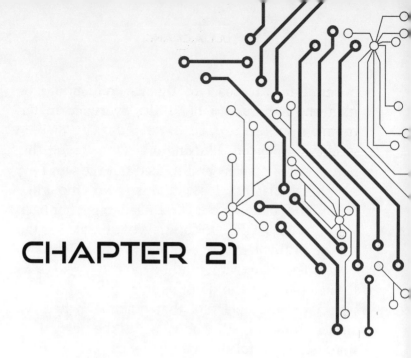

CHAPTER 21

Lucas looked up from his computer, as if he had been concentrating on something important, when Harrington stormed into the room. The man's face was dark red, a vein pulsed on his forehead, and he had balled his hands into fists. The door slammed behind him. "How the hell did this happen?"

"It was always a risk," Lucas said evenly, carefully composing his face into a calm expression. "Why else would we have armed guards and have kept her under lock and key if we didn't see this as a possibility? You give someone that much technology..." Lucas leaned back in his chair and frowned, rubbing his temples. "She must have felt threatened. She is programmed to react to threats. We should be glad she ran instead of killing everyone in the room."

That silenced Harrington. He shoved his hands in his pockets and looked out the window, his eyes distant, lost in his own thoughts. "Dammit!" he burst out. "We need to get her back. Why isn't her GPS working? What the hell is the use of all this technology if it's not even going to work? You realize it would be the end for all of us if the media got ahold of this story."

"We were aware of that potential when we signed on for the job with the extensive nondisclosure forms you made us sign." Lucas leaned forward and tapped on the keyboard. "I'm not sure what's going on. Look at this — the signal shows her still in her room."

Harrington came around the desk and looked over his shoulder. "Could she be back?"

Lucas didn't answer.

"Do you think she was smart enough to reprogram the system to throw us off? Could she have had access to the programs?"

Lucas pushed his seat back and stood up. "You know, I bet that is exactly what happened. I never thought of that. She certainly has enough knowledge stored in her database."

"We made her too well," Harrington mused, bitterly.

"It could just be a glitch. As you know,

computers are not fail proof." Or maybe I helped her escape, Lucas thought wryly.

Ever since he had sounded the alarm, Lucas had been a nervous wreck. In order to keep suspicion off himself, he had to be the one to notify the guards about her escape. After seeing her off into the night, he sounded the alarm.

He had to hide a smile. For Kaitlyn, getting off the compound would have only taken minutes.

Hopefully he had done enough to keep him in the clear.

According to the initial reports, she'd managed to evade the security team so far. At one point, they were on her trail, but lost her. Not even for a second did he doubt her ability to evade capture. He was more worried what would happen once she tried to blend in with civilians.

Harrington paced the room. The burly man looked like he was about to blow a fuse. "I am supposed to renegotiate the terms of the hand off with the secretary of defense. Tomorrow. How in the hell am I going to explain we've lost the package?"

Lucas knew Harrington would find away. He always did.

"You could call and tell them you have to push back the negotiations due to a conflicting schedule," Lucas suggested.

Harrington swiveled and stared at Lucas like he'd lost his mind. "Son, we are talking about the

United States Government. They wait for no one."

"Well, then tell them you are having second thoughts and need more time. This is, after all, a huge commitment for IFICS."

The usually calm and collected Harrington growled with frustration and angrily swiped the pen holder across the desk. It clattered to the ground, pens rolling across the white tile floor. "It looks like I don't have a choice."

Lucas ignored the outburst and went back to his computer. Harrington left the room without another word. Of course, he didn't bother to pick up his mess.

By now, Lucas thought, Kate had access to her memories. He wondered how she handled seeing the traumatic experience that landed her in the hands of IFICS. If only they had more time together before she left, he could have helped her through it.

She was all alone.

God, he wished he could be there for her. No one should have to remember what she went through. He should have told her the police had caught the bastard thanks to the DNA they had pulled from under Kaitlyn's nails. If he ever saw her again, he would make sure she knew she saved other women from being attacked. Not that it would give back the life she lost that night. But her old life was over. She wouldn't have lived on like she had without Lucas and IFICS.

Professor Adams burst through the door, his hangdog face exhausted. He crossed the room, his loafers silent on the tiles, and settled at the desk across from Lucas. Leaning forward on his elbows, he caught Lucas's eye. "Do you know something about her escape?"

Lucas's hand stopped mid-air before he hit the next key stroke. "I can't believe you just asked me that."

The professor sighed and threw his hands up in the air. "I've gone over it a thousand times, Lucas. There is no way she could have gotten out without help." His face hardened and his eyes narrowed at Lucas. "I talked to the guards, and they said you've been spending time with her after work."

"Of course I didn't help her," Lucas said angrily, his heart pounding. "I think you know how important this job is to me. I've given everything to this company." He was surprised at how easily the lies rolled off his tongue.

Professor Adams pushed his glasses back up his nose, shaking his head sadly. "I've seen the way you look at her, Lucas. She seems to have gotten to Quess, too. If you know anything that can help us get her back, you need to tell me. It's not safe out there for her. She needs to be in a controlled environment."

"It's not exactly safe in here for her, either!" Lucas couldn't stop the words from coming, and once they were out, he gritted his teeth.

"What are you saying, Lucas?"

Lucas's gaze automatically flicked to the security camera in the corner of the ceiling, pointed directly at him. "Look, okay. Yes, she got to me," Lucas said, "and yes I liked her. But I didn't help her escape. If I knew where she was, I would tell you. I honestly have no idea. She could be anywhere. She is programmed to be evasive and avoid capture, after all." It was mostly the truth, though Lucas would have said anything to protect her.

The professor waited a beat and remarked, "We could shut her down."

Lucas's heart slammed against his chest. Adams wouldn't seriously do that. He couldn't. "If we shut her down, she'll die."

"But she wouldn't be a danger to anyone. If news of a cyborg came out, and that she—a lethal, tactical machine—was loose in the general population, that would be it. We would all be done. Sent to jail. I'm too old for prison. Don't for a second think that we wouldn't be the fall guys for this debacle. The Department of Defense would point at us and cover their asses."

"We knew the risk when we accepted the job," Lucas said through clenched teeth. "If we shut her down, then who knows who would find her with the GPS off-line? And I don't think Harrington would approve of his hundreds of millions of dollars and technology being thrown away like that."

Adams glanced around the lab. As the heating unit clicked on, he stood and came to sit in a chair nearer to Lucas. In a low voice, he said, "You could convince Harrington. He trusts your judgment. If you told him it was the best course of action, he would listen."

"Forget it. Just give the security team time. I'm sure they can bring her back in."

Adams laughed bitterly. "We both know there is not a chance in hell they can capture her."

Truer words had never been spoken. They would know since they were the ones who made her.

"I'll speak to Harrington myself." Adams dropped his head. He looked older than usual, weary, as if the life was being sucked out of him with every passing second Kaitlyn was gone.

"I wouldn't bother. Harrington is well aware of the options. It will just piss him off. Let him make up his own mind."

"Maybe you're right," Adams said. Perhaps I should just take off. Lord knows I've got enough money saved after all the years here. I'm too old for prison. I have my wife and Quess to think about."

"Don't do anything rash," Lucas told him. "Just give it time to unfold. If it looks like the authorities are going to come after us, then you can act. Just get your affairs in order, but hold steady for now."

"Such a smart young lad you are, Lucas. I'll just stay the course for now. But the first sign of things going south…"

"I don't blame you." Lucas stood up and walked over to the coffee pot to refill his mug. He was tired and knew sleep would not come any time soon.

Keep running, Kate, and don't look back.

"Where would she go? We should be able to figure it out. After all we programmed her." Adams said thoughtfully. "Perhaps we can outthink her and lead a team to her."

Lucas took a sip of his coffee and tried to think of a response. Maybe he could throw them off her trail, but he really had no idea where she would go. Adams wasn't aware she had feelings and now had access to her old memories. Would she return to her old home? Lucas didn't think so. At least not right away.

"I have no idea where she would go. It could be a huge city that she could meld into or find a cave in the middle of the woods. I'm afraid none of us can think like Kaitlyn even if we did program her. Her software is so advanced our minds couldn't begin to keep up."

"I suppose you're right." Adams grumbled under his breath. "I just wish we could find a way to fix this disaster, before it comes back to haunt us."

Taking another sip of his coffee, Lucas remained silent.

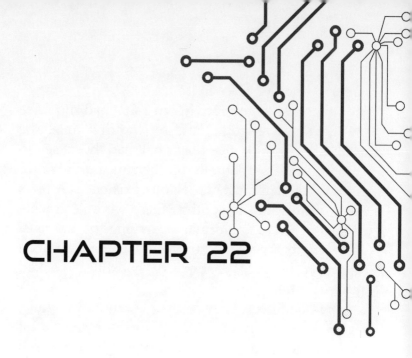

CHAPTER 22

The sun was starting to rise. Kaitlyn had managed to evade capture on two different occasions. For now, she was in the clear.

Her internal clock informed her she was only twenty-three minutes from civilization if she kept the same pace. The thought brought a sense of relief, along with a pang of fear and she anxiously tugged her sleeves down to her wrists. Even though the clothes covered her irregularities, she still felt self-conscious. Maybe she wouldn't be able to pull off being human. What if people could tell just by looking at her that she wasn't normal.

She couldn't help but wonder what kind of strange new world lay ahead. Would she ever be able to find her place in it?

Once she got into town, she had no idea where she was going, and for the first time, she started to doubt the plan that had been set in motion. Life perpetually on the run didn't sound much better than her previous existence. After a scan of the area to confirm there were no threats nearby, just the normal scurrying of animals, Kaitlyn dropped to the ground and rummaged through the bag. What exactly had Lucas packed away for her?

He had been planning her escape for a while, it seemed. A driver's license, passport, and a lot of cash. Kaitlyn studied the drivers license, Sarah Granger. So she was supposed to start over with a new name. Sarah, she played the name over in her mind, and decided she didn't like the name at all. The ID had her address in Colorado. Maybe that's where she should go.

She pulled out a navy baseball cap and glasses. She was impressed. Frank had drilled in her head it was the little details that matter the most. The props would help her blend in, become invisible.

Kaitlyn twisted her hair into a ponytail, lowered the hat on her head, and slid on the eyeglasses. It would be enough of a disguise to get her by—for now. Just in case they had police looking for her, which she doubted. They wouldn't want to draw attention to her. To be on the safe side, she knew she should cut her hair and change the color when she figured out where she was going. Lucas had said to trust her instincts. Easier said than done. Her mind worked on logic, not instinct.

Once again, her thoughts drifted to her new memories. She couldn't stop thinking about the woman who had been raped. Was she okay? Was the attacker...her murderer...caught?? For some reason, knowing her old life had ended trying to save someone else made her feel better than if she had been in a car accident. She had no idea why she felt that way. Feelings and emotions were so confusing. She wished there was some kind of manual to help her sort through them.

Time to move. Kaitlyn continued on the path and soon broke out onto a main highway. She jumped over the railing and strode forward, whipping out the phone and consulting the map. The nearest town was only three miles down the road. Once she got there, she would have to find transportation to get further away. She had to put as much distance between her and the compound as possible. Eventually, she would need to rest. She didn't want to over-stress her system. She could technically last for days without sleep, but Lucas had told her it was better to get periodic breaks as long as she wasn't in danger.

A dark sedan pulled over and an older man leaned out the window. "Need a lift, sweetheart?"

Caution. Unsure how to respond, Kaitlyn ignored him and kept walking. The man pulled away and continued down the road. Ahead there was a sign that said Maryville, population 1725.

When the town came into view, Kaitlyn wondered if she would be able to pull it off. She had never interacted with anyone outside of the compound before. It wasn't much of a town from what she could see. A few houses lined the street, with a run-down gas station on one side, across from a diner with a flashing arrow.

Kaitlyn pushed open the door into the gas station. A bell went off above her head and she tensed. Was that a warning?

"Morning, dear." A plump woman with a nice smile and grey hair greeted her. The badge on her shirt said her name was Marcy.

"Good morning," Kaitlyn replied.

"Can I help you with something? You look a little lost."

Great. Her first interaction, and they already knew she was lost. "Is there a train station or bus stop anywhere close?"

"Sure is. There's a Greyhound about three miles up the road, and you can take that to connect to Alexandria Union Station. Where are you headed?"

"Fort Lauderdale, Florida." Kaitlyn frowned and wondered why those words slipped out of her mouth. Somewhere deep in her subconscious, she knew that was where she was supposed to be. She wished she could take back the words once they escaped. The security team would probably come looking for her and ask if anyone had seen someone matching her description. She could kill the lady, but that seemed harsh. If they followed her to Florida she would just have to loose them.

"Well, that's quite the trip. You might want to grab a few snacks."

Humans ate all the time, she reminded herself. If she wanted to blend in, she had to act the part.

"You're right," she said, smiling. "I'm starving."

She made her way to the back of the store and grabbed a couple of bags of chips and two candy bars. When she reached for the Butterfingers, a memory crossed her mind. She looked to be around twelve years old, and she was rummaging through a plastic pumpkin filled with candy, searching for Butterfingers.

A slow smile spread across her face. She was starting to welcome the memories. It was like pieces of a jigsaw puzzle slowly fitting together. Once she had all the pieces, she would have a clear image of who she used to be.

"Don't forget to grab a drink." Marcy tilted her head towards the cooler.

Right. Can't forget a drink, Kaitlyn thought wryly as she reached in for a bottle of water.

"That will be seven dollars and ninety-nine

cents."

Kaitlyn stood there confused for a moment until her processor flashed money. She scrabbled through her bag and pulled out her money and dropped a hundred dollar bill on the counter.

Marcy eyed the bill. "Don't you have anything smaller than that?"

Kaitlyn flipped through her bills; she really should have researched more. Finally, she found one that had the number ten on it and handed that to the woman.

"Thanks, that's better. And be careful flashing that kind of money around. The world is filled with bad people." The woman handed her money back which Kaitlyn stuffed into the side pocket of her bag.

"Bad people?" Kate asked.

"Don't you watch the news?"

She shook her head no. "I only watch movies."

The woman was looking at her strangely, and Kate realized she said something wrong to draw attention to herself.

"Thanks for the advice. I'll be more careful from now on." Kaitlyn turned to exit the building.

"Have a safe trip."

"Thank you." Kaitlyn could understand why the IFICS were concerned about her interacting with humans; she wasn't very good at it. She felt like a fish out of water. The saying had just popped into her head, an element of the slang chip, she suspected. It reminded her of Quess and made her feel strange. She didn't have time to analyze feelings; she had to get to the bus station.

It was as if she were set on autopilot. At the bus station, a kind-faced gentleman in a uniform helped her find the right bus.

She boarded the bus and made her way to the back. She wanted to be able to see who entered, and also she had quick access to the emergency exit.

The memory of the attack kept playing through her mind as she watched the scenery pass. The bus rolled down the highway in the early morning, once in awhile they past quiet little towns. She couldn't stop thinking of the the woman at the gas station's words—*bad people*. Why was there so much wicked in the world? What would make someone want to hurt a defenseless woman?

Kaitlyn scanned her information drive and was appalled to see that in the United States alone over 1.2 million incidents of violent crimes were reported yearly. Over 90,000 of those incidents involved rape.

She stewed over the statistics for many miles, and it fueled her desire to make the world a better place. Could one person really have that much of an impact? One less woman being abused would be something.

Without being obvious she observed the passengers. It was interesting to see people outside the setting of the compound. She wondered if anyone on the bus had been a victim of a crime, or if there were criminals on board. More than likely there were both.

There was a young couple sitting diagonal from her. They didn't seem to be very happy. The young woman had her arms crossed against her chest and the man stared out the window. She wondered if they were in a fight and if so what about? She felt a pang of loneliness for Lucas. She would probably never see him again.

An old lady sat across from Kaitlyn. She pulled yarn out of her bag and started knitting. Kaitlyn watched her old hands move at a rapid pace. Kaitlyn was fascinated as the yarn started to become a large square.

The old woman caught her eye and smiled.

"Do you knit?"

Startled Kate shook her head no.

"It's relaxing. Helps make the time pass. I could teach you if you want."

"No, thank you."

The woman shrugged and went back to her knitting.

Maybe she could fit in. So far no one had treated her differently. Other than some gross guy with a mustache that kept turning to leer at her. Doing a scan Kaitlyn realized the man was sexually aroused. The thought repulsed her. She wanted to use a pressure point to make the man pass out, but she knew that was not a good idea. She didn't need to draw attention to herself in the enclosed environment.

Why Fort Lauderdale? Why couldn't she remember if it was her home?

In Alexandria, she switched to the train without incident. The further south they went the less the leaves had changed. The stunning red, golds and orange turned to all green. She watched the sun set and rise again from her window seat.

She dozed off with her head against the cool window and dreamed of Evan. Only this time, the dreams were more than just flashes. They were complete scenes. They had been in love; that much was obvious.

Kaitlyn woke up from a particularly vivid Christmas memory. She had just been about to open a small package from Evan, her cheeks flushed with happiness. She searched her memories but couldn't find that one.

As the train drifted into the station, she wondered what it meant that she was dreaming and thinking of Evan when her heart ached for Lucas.

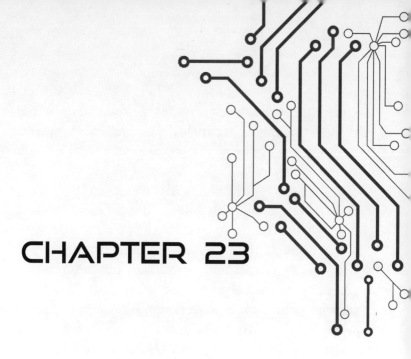

CHAPTER 23

After twenty-one hours on the road, between trains stops and layovers, the train finally pulled into the station. She was certain she hadn't been followed. Search teams were probably still combing the woods for her.

When Kaitlyn got off the train in Fort Lauderdale, she had a feeling she had been there before.

Could her instincts have taken her home? The thought scared her. What was she going to do, just waltz back into her old life?

She was way beyond that point.

Maybe she could get back on the train and go further south, or even west. But there was something about the coast line that was drawing her in, so she shouldered her bag and started walking. Palm trees lined the road. For some reason this made her miss Quess, and their walks. A palm tree could never replace her favorite birch tree.

Kaitlyn wandered down the highway, following the signs that said "Beach". She crossed a large bridge. Cars whizzed by, and a few of them honked their horns. She had no idea what that meant. The smell of the salt air tugged at a memory. She was getting fragments, but nothing strong and overpowering like the earlier memories. She must have spent a lot of time near the ocean in her past life, which would explain the pull.

A parking lot edged up against the sand, and Kaitlyn mounted the long boardwalk that led down to the beach. Neon lights ran down the length of the boardwalk. People sat on the edging, bikers road by and few people skated past her.

She left the sidewalk and stepped onto the sandy beach. The grey-blue ocean spread before her beneath a sky of white, fluffy clouds. There were couples walking hand in hand or sitting on blankets near the water while their children made sand castles. Kaitlyn pulled off her shoes and stepped barefoot onto the warm, gritty sand, making a straight line for the water. No one gave her a second glance. For the first time in her new life she felt invisible. She was just another person enjoying the beach. The thought was comforting, even though she knew it was far from the truth. She would never be truly human again.

It felt so natural to step into the surf. The ocean waves lapping against the sand and her feet had a calming effect on her. Almost like the way Lucas calmed her mind.

She noticed some people were sleeping on the beach, and she wondered if she should do that as well, but her sensors flashed Caution. After a quick scan, she realized she needed to find a hotel. Reluctantly, Kaitlyn made her way across the beach and back to the main road.

Several hotels lined the street, many of them flashing Vacancy signs. She entered the first hotel and greeted the clerk behind the counter.

"I would like to stay the night, please," Kaitlyn said.

"Of course." The older woman turned to her computer and started clicking on the keyboard. "One night will be ninety-seven."

Kaitlyn reached in her bag and handed the clerk a hundred.

"No, sorry. We need a credit card to keep on file."

Kaitlyn stared at her blankly.

"A credit card. You know, the plastic card with one of these symbols." The clerk pointed at a sign on the counter.

Kaitlyn's scans recognized the five colorful

emblems. Within seconds, she knew what each stood for and she knew she didn't have one.

"I don't have one of those," she said, holding out the hundred dollar bill. "I only have cash."

"Company policy. No card, no room."

Kaitlyn shoved the money back in the side pocket of her bag before she slung it on her shoulders. "Do you know of any hotels in the area that don't require credit cards?" she asked stiffly.

"Sorry, dear. Those kinds of no-tell-motels are across the bridge on the bad side of town."

Why did everyone keep saying bad? Bad people. Bad side of town.

Kaitlyn pushed the glass door open and stepped back outside. She didn't need to sleep, but her body needed to recharge, and if she stayed awake too long it would drain her energy. And when she was on the run, that wasn't ideal. She needed to find a place to rest for the night. She also needed to find a change of clothes.

Follow your instincts.

Kaitlyn walked, letting her feet take her wherever they wandered. Off the main highway and deep into a residential part of town, she passed colorful Spanish-themed houses with brilliant green lawns beneath the spray of sprinklers.

She had been wandering for two hours when a wave of familiarity washed over her. She had been here before. The sun had set and the street lights came to life.

She turned left down Green Street and walked to the end of the cul-de-sac. Without a thought, she came to a stop in front of a large white stucco home. The porch light was on, and lamps glowed from several windows. She stared at the wooden swing on the porch, and images flashed before her—sitting on the swing with her parents, and later, with Evan. This house had been her home. Her body tingled with excitement. Her parents were behind the door.

She fought the urge to run up the stairs and ring the doorbell. It would be cruel to come back from the dead. Her parents would never understand. Her excitement quickly turned to overwhelming sadness.

Kaitlyn hung her head and spun on the ball of her foot, leaving without a single glance back.

On autopilot, Kaitlyn took a left down Sanders and a right down Oakwood Drive. Evan. Her body was pulling her to Evan. She wanted to resist, but her feet kept moving forward. Just one peek. She wanted to see him, she had to, and then she would leave.

She was watching the pavement, lost in her own thoughts, when she heard laughter. She looked up to find a couple walking towards her— a blond-haired guy and a beautiful blonde girl.

Kaitlyn's body revved up, and just as quickly her body stabilized as her sensors overrode the fight or flight impulse.

Evan.

Her eyes met his, and she forced her face to stay blank.

"Cassidy?" His voice was incredulous. He abruptly let go of the woman and stepped forward.

Cassidy. Not only had the IFICS taken her old life, they had given her a new name.

"Excuse me?" Kaitlyn pulled her hat down lower.

He was silent for a long time, his girlfriend shifting uncomfortably behind him, and Kaitlyn in front, standing still, her heart hammering.

"I'm sorry." He shook his head, his face pale. "You look like someone I once knew."

Kaitlyn covertly scanned Evan and was surprised to see he had a wedding band on his left hand. She glanced over at the blonde—she wore a matching band. Kaitlyn gritted her teeth; he hadn't wasted any time moving on. She kept her face expressionless.

"It's uncanny, really. The resemblance." Evan's face looked pained. "It's like seeing a ghost."

The blonde woman came up and grabbed his hand, squeezing it. "Sorry, sweetie," she said. Addressing Kaitlyn, she added, "He lost someone once. Any girl with dark hair and your build always stops him in his tracks."

"It's okay." Kaitlyn was proud when her own voice didn't waver. "I saw a movie once where they said everyone has a twin."

"We should go, babe," the blonde murmured to Evan.

Evan's eyes were glued to Kaitlyn's face. It was making her uncomfortable.

"Your friend's name was Cassidy?" Kaitlyn asked the question before she lost her nerve. "What happened to her, if you don't mind me asking?"

"She was murdered. A long time ago."

A long time ago? Kaitlyn opened her mouth to ask "how long?" but Evan spoke again, turning to his wife. "The resemblance really is uncanny, isn't it, Rachel?"

The woman nodded in agreement, her sapphire gaze regarding Kaitlyn seriously. "Yes. It is eerie. Come on, babe. Let's leave this poor girl alone. We're sorry to bother you."

Kaitlyn nodded but didn't say anything more as the woman took hold of Evan's arm and pulled him past her. She could smell his cologne as he passed, his eyes catching hers one last time. Kaitlyn breathed deeply; the scent was so familiar. She continued down the sidewalk, her hands still shaking from the encounter.

How could he have replaced her so quickly? He was married?

Something wasn't right. Quess had said Evan

was twenty-one, and it had bothered Kaitlyn at the time, but she wasn't sure why. If she was only seventeen, had her parents let her date a twenty-one year old? A cursory scan of state laws told her that was illegal.

She was murdered. A long time ago.

How long?

Kaitlyn waited until Evan and the blonde had turned a corner and were out of sight, then she took off at a steady run. Lucas had warned her she was faster than humans, and she needed to be careful not to draw attention to herself. A six mile per hour pace seemed adequate. She ran through the streets and came to a stop before the first store she found. The store had bars on the windows. She had obviously ventured into the bad side of town.

Taking a deep breath, Kaitlyn walked through the door and grabbed a soda and some beef jerky. After she paid the cashier, she asked, "What is today?"

"Monday. All day it's been Monday."

Kate shook her head. "I mean the date and year."

The older woman looked at her through narrowed eyes. "Are you being fresh with me, child?"

"No. I was in an accident and sometimes I forget things."

"Oh, you poor thing. Amnesia?"

Kate scanned the definition and nodded. "Yes, ma'am. Amnesia."

"It's the twenty-eighth of September, 2014."

Kate wobbled on her feet, but managed to compose herself before the cashier noticed her panic. The mechanism that overrode her balance set in place, whirled, and she felt better.

Twenty-fourteen.

"Thank you." Kaitlyn turned towards the door, her thoughts clouded.

"Honey." The cashier pushed the bag over the counter, her dark eyes concerned. "You forgot your bag."

Kaitlyn thanked her, grabbed the bag, and nearly ran from the building. She stopped on the sidewalk, the hot sun beating down on her. Her world had tilted.

Three years had passed since her accident. Not several months, like she had thought. Where did that time go?

Kaitlyn needed answers, and there was only one person who could give them to her.

Lucas.

Her mind was racing. How could this be? She was so distracted she didn't notice the group of guys up ahead. She heard someone whistle and her head snapped up, and she stopped in her tracks.

"My my, what's a girl like you doing on this side of town? Slumming?"

Slumming? She didn't respond. There were four of them, and she didn't need her sensors to know they were going to be trouble. She really wasn't in the mood.

"Cat got your tongue?"

"Why would a cat have my tongue?" She asked innocently even though, thanks to the slang chip, she knew it was yet another human saying that made no sense.

"Comedian. We got a funny girl." A tall guy with tattoos all over his muscular arms, and neck stepped forward. The leader. His chest was puffed up like a rooster.

"I don't want any trouble." Kaitlyn said calmly. In her mind she was going over avenues of attack.

"Well, sweetheart you are on the wrong side of the tracks. Trouble is all you find over here."

"That's a shame. You shouldn't let a train track decide if you are good or bad."

A couple of the guys laughed in the background.

"Feisty, I like it."

"What's your name?" Kaitlyn asked.

"What's it to you?"

"I'd like to know your name before I kick your ass."

"You and what army. I'll tell you what's going to happen." He flicked a knife out of his pocket. "I'm going to tear your clothes off, and then make you beg for it. Once I'm done with you, my boys are going to have their turn."

"I don't think so." Kaitlyn, felt her body relax. She welcomed the chance to take out her anger on these jerks. Her mind flashed back to the girl that was raped and the man who caused the end of her life and the start of her new one. As far as she was concerned, the world would be a better place with four less bullies. Someone had to teach them a lesson, and it might as well be her.

The guy licked his lips and took a step forward.

In a blur Kaitlyn slammed her elbow into the crook of his arm. The knife clattered to the ground. Kaitlyn kicked it away. The guy's eyes widened in surprise. The other three moved forward, but the tough guy waved them away.

"I got this bitch." He snarled, his eyes flashed with anger.

He lunged forward, and Kate side stepped causing him to loose his footing. Kate took the advantage and slammed the heel of her open palm into his chest as he fell forward. She heard his ribs crack. He fell to the ground coughing blood. The three guys looked at each other.

A stocky bald guy of average height and wide shoulders came forward. She found it funny that they came one at time when they would have had a better chance if all three attacked. Not much of a chance, but still.

Kaitlyn got into position with her legs bent making it easier to pivot and deliver strikes to her opponent. The guy cocked back his arm and threw a wild punch which Kate deflected easily. She sensed the guy on the ground move, but she knew he wasn't a threat.

Go to your opponent, Frank had told her. Never show fear. Move forward. Don't hesitate; they wont expect it. The grueling hours of training had paid off. She acted reflexively.

Pivoting on the balls of her feet, Kaitlyn delivered a swift kick to his larynx, crushing his wind pipe. The guy dropped to his knees and grabbed his throat. She advanced towards the last two, but they took off in a sprint. She could chase them down, but she had a train to catch.

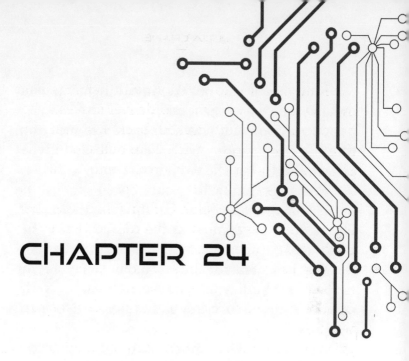

CHAPTER 24

Once again, Kaitlyn was on a train headed back in the direction she had come from.

Anger filled her so completely that she couldn't see past the rage. Lies. She was sick of all the lies. After all IFICS had taken from her, she deserved the truth. The decision had been so easy to make. There was nothing left of her old life but memories. She couldn't return to her parents and their white house, and Evan had moved on with his life. They could not accept her for the robot she had become. She couldn't expect them to. If her parents found out what had happened to her. Lucas and the others would all go to jail. She needed to speak to Lucas first. Perhaps someday she would find a way to come back to her parents, but right now it was not the time. Life had moved on when she was gone.

So Kate knew it was time for her to move on, too. She wasn't sure where she would go or what she would do, but she would start over.

Remembering what Lucas said about the handheld device, Kaitlyn reached for the phone. She noticed the symbol at the top informing her that the battery was getting low.

She hesitated for only a moment before she tapped the button and spoke as clearly as she could. "Lucas Andrews address. Northern Virginia."

Kaitlyn actually smiled. A robot talking to a robot.

A list of potential addresses scrolled across the phone, and Kaitlyn was impressed. She narrowed it down to three locations, and turned off the phone to conserve the battery.

She didn't notice the scenery or the passengers this time. Her sole focus was finding out what had happened to her lost time. She knew going back was dangerous. They would be looking for her. They might even be watching Lucas, but she had to chance it. She had to know.

She dozed off, and for the first time since she could recall, she didn't dream about Evan.

As the train pulled into the station, she grabbed her bag and wondered about the significance of this change. Maybe seeing him in person and knowing he had accepted her death and moved on had allowed her to close that part of her subconscious. She still couldn't get over the fact that he was married, or that her real name was Cassidy. But the most mind-boggling was the time that had passed. Where had that time gone?

It was cool as she made her way out into the early morning. She didn't notice it of course, but her internal thermometer flashed fifty-seven degrees. The station bustled with commuters coming and going, and she stopped to watch for a moment. So many people going about their day, living their normal lives. She saw a man wearing a suit carrying a briefcase. He looked like he was talking to himself, but she noticed he was speaking into an bluetooth earpiece. A long line at the coffee cart. A woman pulled her sweater tighter in the brisk air. They had no idea a freak, a deadly super soldier, walked amongst them.

Switching on the phone, she browsed the map function. It took Kaitlyn almost an hour to reach the first potential address by foot. There was an older model Cadillac in the driveway, so unless Lucas lived with someone, she had a feeling this would be a bust. Although, with the way things were going, even that wouldn't surprise her at this point.

She rang the doorbell, and an older man answered.

Smiling brightly, Kaitlyn asked, "Excuse me, is Lucas home?"

The man stared at her for a long moment before answering. "Nope. Lucas is at his friends house. What do you want with him?"

Her mind raced, trying to come up with a plausible explanation. Finally, she just went with the truth. "It was a shot in the dark. My ex-boyfriend's name is Lucas Andrews. I looked him up, and this was one of the addresses."

The man tsked. "Damn computers can tell you anything nowadays. Sorry, wrong house, I'm afraid. I think my Lucas is a bit too young for you. Good luck on your search." He shut the door.

Following her instincts, Kaitlyn skipped the second name on the list and made her way to the third, even though it was further away. Something in the back of her mind told her it was the location she was searching for. When she checked the map, it gave her the distances when walking and for when traveling by car. She decided to grab a cab like they always did in the movies. After standing on the street for ten minutes, she realized the chances of catching a cab on a side street in the suburbs were not very good, so navigated to the main highway.

The first time a yellow cab rode by, she stuck out her hand, but it drove past her. She had no idea what she was doing wrong.

About ten minutes later, another came down

the highway, and pulled over. She slid in the front seat and showed the driver the address on her phone. The car pulled out and neither spoke on the drive, which was fine by her. She wasn't feeling chatty.

"Please drive past the house without stopping."

The driver raised an eyebrow, but kept driving.

Kaitlyn recognized Lucas's Jeep in the driveway. She stared up at the small brick house. Hopefully, he didn't have a secret wife she wasn't aware of.

"Can you drop me off two blocks ahead?"

The driver drove ahead without a word. She noticed a black SUV parked across the street from Lucas's.

Walking casually she turned right and then left, and walked the two blocks until she was directly behind Lucas's house a street over. She should wait till nightfall, but she wanted answers now.

Harrington's security team wasn't that large. More than likely there was only one guard watching the house and he would never see her enter.

She walked through the yard and hopped the short chain linked fence. As she suspected, there was no one in the back yard. She hurried up the back steps, and knocked on the door.

The door swung open, and Lucas stood, staring at her, his mouth agape. He was only wearing plaid pajama bottoms and nothing else. The sight of his bare skin almost made her forget what she was there for.

"Kate?" He pulled her into the dim interior and slammed the door. "What are you...how did you...what are you doing here? There's a guard out front."

"That's why I came in the back door." She looked away from his chest and met his eyes. "Why Lucas? Why all the lies?"

"Come in here and sit down. What's happened?"

He led her into an open living room. Dark curtains were drawn and the lights were out. A worn leather couch faced a brick fire place, and a large red rug covered the hardwood floor beneath a coffee table. The walls were lined with bookshelves. A brushed metal lamp sat on a dark wooden end table. Her mind was going through the stores where they were purchased, but she ignored it. She didn't care where Lucas shopped. She wanted different answers.

"Sit down." Lucas motioned to the couch.

A black cat with a white patch of fur around its left eye strolled slowly into the room and sat down, flicking her tail as she stared suspiciously at Kate. She wondered if it could tell she wasn't fully human.

"How old am I, Lucas, and... you have a cat?"

He settled in a recliner next to the couch and dropped his head. "You're twenty, and yes, I have a cat. She came with the house, I guess you could say."

The cat seemed to make some kind of decision, and jumped on Kate's lap. Startled, she ran her hand down its soft fur without really thinking about it.

"Domino never goes to anyone."

"Domino?"

"The cat. She's very much a loner."

"Kindred souls, I guess. Why did you let me believe I was seventeen?"

Lucas sighed. "I guess I never thought about your age. I didn't realize you thought about your age."

"I don't care about my age. What I want to know is what happened to me in those lost years?"

Lucas leaned forward to take her hand, but she pulled away. His brow knitted together. "You were in a coma for almost three years."

Kaitlyn didn't say anything for a long time while she processed the new information. "I remember waking up and seeing you."

"Do you?" He smiled sadly. "I sat by your bed every day. We weren't sure you would pull through. It's a miracle you're alive."

"A miracle, or science?"

He shrugged. "They often go hand in hand."

"I'm so confused, Lucas. I thought it would help, finding out who I was, but it hasn't helped at all." She stared at him. "I saw someone from my past. Someone I once loved."

Lucas tensed. "Evan."

Nodding, she replied, "I saw Evan, and that made me even more confused."

"What happened?"

"Don't worry. I didn't tell him anything. He just thought I was someone that looked like Cassidy. My name is Cassidy? That doesn't even sound right."

"It was Cassidy," Lucas said gently. "You're Kaitlyn now. Unless you want to be Cassidy?"

She shook her head. "No. Cassidy died a long time ago."

"How did you feel when you met him?" Lucas looked away as if he didn't really want to hear the answer.

"Strange. He's married now. I didn't feel a pull towards him the way I thought I would, the way I do with you."

Lucas's shoulders relaxed, and Kaitlyn realized he had been jealous.

"You have nothing to worry about, Lucas." She didn't know why she was comforting him after all the lies.

"Why are you back? You should have kept

running. Everyone is looking for you. If they find out you were here…"

"I don't want to run," Kaitlyn cut in wearily. "Run to where? I had a lot of time to think on the train."

"Tell me what you want, Kate, and I will do everything in my power to make it happen."

"I thought about the woman that was raped. Cassidy was brave and wanted to help others. I want to honor the girl I used to be. I have all of these upgrades and skills that I could put to use. There is so much bad in the world, maybe I can help. Even if just a little. This is who I am, Lucas, and we should use it for good."

He leaned forward, his elbows resting on his knees. "We can't hand you over, they'll just use you as a weapon. I need to think this over. If we can get Harrington to keep you… I just have to make him understand. We'll have to tell him that you have emotions and your own thoughts, Kate."

"That's fine. I'm sick of hiding who I am. I'm sick of all the lies."

He stood, coming to sit beside her, his hands gently cupping her face as if she were made of glass. "If we can't convince Harrington, we'll run away together. I'm not losing you again, Kate. I was going crazy without you."

"Promise?"

"I promise." He tugged her into a tight hug,

resting his head on hers as she leaned into him. The cat jumped off her lap and ran out of the room.

"I need a shower and change of clothes. But right now, I just want to sit here with you, if that's okay?" Kaitlyn asked.

"More than okay."

"Has the guard entered the house?"

"No, he just sits out there all day and night. They switch shifts at nine."

"Useless."

"I think it makes Harrington feel like he's doing something. He's going crazy."

She pulled away to look into his eyes. "Can we wait till tomorrow to talk to Harrington?"

"Absolutely." Lucas entwined his hand in Kaitlyn's and slowly rubbed his thumb along her knuckles. "Anything for you. Besides it's Sunday anyway."

When he leaned down and kissed her, Kaitlyn sank against him, comforted by his presence, the feel of his chest beneath her fingertips. It had been a long couple of days, and in the end, she was where she belonged.

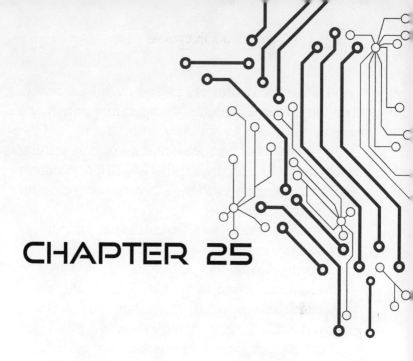

CHAPTER 25

Lucas whistled as he tossed Kaitlyn's clothes in the washing machine and dumped a cup of detergent inside. Everything will be okay, he told himself. Somehow, they would work it out. He wouldn't hesitate to run away with Kate if that was what it came down to, and that fact alone brought a sense of calm to him. He would do anything to keep her safe.

Even if it meant walking away from everything he knew.

He paused, staring at the way the leftover detergent pooled in the bottom of the cup. Wasn't that exactly what they had done to her? They had stripped her of everything that made her 'Cassidy' the night she lost her life.

Out of the corner of his eye, he saw her walk into the kitchen. She was wrapped in a grey towel that matched her eyes… and nothing else. Just the sight caused his heart to pound and his breathing to change. He put the cap back on the detergent and shut the door to the washer, but forgot to hit Start.

"Feel better?" he asked, unable to tear his gaze away.

Her hair was wet and tousled. She looked fresh-faced and innocent. Gone was the blank stare he had expected from her for so long, replaced with a look of wide-eyed wonder. She had been stuck on the compound for so long, it must have been such a stark contrast to be free, to see all the things, the knick knacks and belongings that make up a person's home. Freedom looked so unlike her bland room on the compound. He wanted to be the one to share in her newfound freedom. There was so much for her to explore and learn. He smiled at the thought of being by her side to experience it with her.

The sight of her bare shoulders was too much. The way she clutched the towel pushed her breasts up, spilling cleavage over the top. His mind started speeding down a road he knew should be left alone. At least for now. She wasn't ready to take their relationship to that level. Not yet.

He cleared his throat. "I left you some clothes

in the bathroom."

"I saw them." She smiled sweetly and crossed the room until she was a few feet away.

Without another word, Kaitlyn dropped the towel and stood before him, unflinching. There wasn't a hint of modesty or self-consciousness. She was breathtaking. Her body was strong and yet still feminine with curves that begged to be touched.

Lucas clenched his hands, focusing on deep breaths as his body responded to her. "Kate, what are you doing?"

She stepped forward, her clean citrusy scent wafting towards him, and spoke in a low voice. "When you returned my memories, I found out I wasn't a virgin. I know you were concerned about that. So I thought we could have sex now. If you wanted to. I want to see what it feels like. I can't remember."

Lucas closed his eyes and then opened them, sweeping his gaze over her. He couldn't believe what he was seeing. "My God, you are stunning," he whispered.

"You don't find me repulsive?"

"Of course not. It's who you are Kate. You take my breath away."

Slowly, she took a couple more steps forward.

He should probably stop it, but he really didn't want to. Any self-control had gone out the window when the towel had hit the floor. Her fingertips touched his check. Lucas stared into her grey eyes. The color of storm clouds, he thought as he grabbed her hand from his face and moved it to his lips. He gently kissed her palm, and then each finger, relishing the way she shivered beneath his touch.

She closed the distance between them, running her hands up his arms. Her firm, naked body pressed against his, and heat radiated throughout his body.

"Not here. Upstairs," he said roughly.

He entwined his hand with hers and showed her the way. He had wanted her for so long; he still couldn't believe it was coming true.

His bedroom was cool, a window open to the fall breeze as sunshine spilled through the open curtains. Thankfully, his room was on the backside of the house.

He turned to face her, fighting the urge, he willed himself to put the breaks on. "Are you sure? I'm willing to wait as long as it takes. We don't have to rush into this."

"More than sure."

His palms were clammy and his breathing erratic. He was nervous. Never in his life had he wanted anything more than he wanted Kaitlyn, and he was afraid he would mess things up. He pushed the thought aside and hesitantly wrapped his arms around her. He waited, giving her plenty of opportunity to change her mind. When she didn't, he pulled her body to his. Her arms snaked around his neck, and she pressed her bare chest against his.

Lightly, he trailed his lips down her throat to the hollow of her neck and down the gentle curve of her bare shoulder. A gasp escaped her full lips. He was the luckiest man alive.

His heart felt like it was going to jump out of his chest. Her hands moved up his stomach and every nerve in his body felt electrified. He breathed in the scent of her; she smelled citrusy and clean, like his shampoo. He wanted to bury his head in her hair and get lost forever.

Kaitlyn reached for his pajama bottoms, her hands brushing over his skin which caused him to groan as she tugged off his pants. Desire shot through him. Stepping out of his pants, Lucas walked her backwards to the bed and gently pushed her down onto the mattress. He climbed on top of her. His lips found hers, his hand trailing down her side. Kaitlyn arched her back, and he thought he was going to go insane. He moved his hand up her inner thigh, her skin velvet underneath his fingertips, and he felt her body tense.

He paused. "Are you okay? Do you want me to stop?"

Kaitlyn bit the inside of her mouth, and her face was flushed. "What if I don't know how to do it? I wasn't programmed for this."

"No, you certainly weren't," Lucas laughed softly. He rolled off her and propped himself up on one arm. He traced his finger on the full curve of her hip, his body tightening as her gaze moved over him, hunger in her eyes. "You weren't programmed to want to be with me, either, Kate, but here we are. There's an attraction between us that even science couldn't destroy."

Without another word, Kate pulled his head towards hers and brushed her lips softly against his. She climbed on top of him, her hair spilling down onto his chest as she captured his lips. His hands trembled as he ran them up her strong thighs, pulling her hips to settle on his. Their bodies locked together—flesh on flesh. Kaitlyn gasped, her body tensing.

Lucas cupped her breasts in his hands, his pulse in his throat. He could hear his own heart pounding in his ears as she leaned down and kissed him, and their bodies began to move together.

For hours, they explored each other. Outside the window, the sun disappeared and the room fell into darkness. When they came up for air, Kaitlyn's cheeks were rosy, her eyes shining.

They lay entwined together. Lucas waited for his breathing to return to normal.

"Wow," she murmured, her head cradled in the curve of his shoulder.

He kissed her head. "I told you, you had

nothing to worry about. You're incredible."

"You enjoyed it?" Kate asked shyly.

"Are you kidding me? Couldn't you tell." Lucas ran his hand through her long hair. "What about you?"

"Even more amazing than I imagined." Kaitlyn sighed, twisting to look up at him. Her body slid against his, and desire built between them again. "All my senses were hyper-alert. I couldn't think about anything but you."

"I can't get enough of you," Lucas agreed, sliding his palm over her abdomen.

"Can this last forever?" she whispered, kissing him. "Let's never leave this bed."

"As much as I'd like to say yes..." Lucas chuckled.

"I still have so much to learn..." He recognized the devious glint in her grey eyes as she rolled on top of him. "I think I'll have to keep practicing."

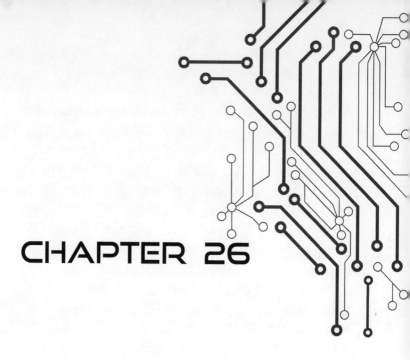

CHAPTER 26

Sunlight filtered through the blinds. Kaitlyn loved the weight of Lucas's arm wrapped loosely around her waist as he slept. She breathed in his wonderful musky smell, running her palm over his bare chest.

They had stayed up most of the night, unable to keep their hands off each other. The evening had been magical. She had been worried that the removal of pain sensors were linked somehow to pleasure, but it certainly seemed that was not the case. At least, not where Lucas was concerned.

A shrill ring broke through the calm silence and Lucas jerked awake. He reached for his phone on the nightstand, accidentally knocked a book to the floor in the process. "Hello," he said hoarsely.

Kaitlyn shifted away as Lucas sat up and looked anxious.

"Yeah, you woke me. What's up? I'm not due in to work for a couple of hours." He smiled reassuringly at Kate, caressing her arm as he listened on the phone.

She felt a charge of electricity run through her anytime his skin touched hers. She knew she could face anything with Lucas by her side.

"I don't think that's a good idea," he said. "Can you come to my house? There's something I would like to talk to you about in person. It's private, and I'd rather discuss it here. Alone."

He clenched his jaw. "I know I work for you and not the other way around. Believe me, you will want to hear this. It's about Kaitlyn, but I'll only talk to you at my house."

Kaitlyn watched the play of emotions cross his face as his eyebrows knitted together. Every move he made fascinated her.

"I wouldn't ask if it wasn't important. I know how valuable your time is."

Another pause. Kaitlyn wondered if it was Harrington on the other end.

"An hour is fine. Your time won't be wasted." Lucas ended the call and rubbed his eyes. "Harrington is coming. I think it's best if we talk to him on our turf, not his. I don't want him to have the chance to lock you away before he hears us out." His heart rate was increased and his body was tense.

"What was he calling about?" Kaitlyn scooted up and laid her head on his shoulder.

"He wants to have a meeting to see if we should shut down the project since you haven't been found."

Her eyes widened. "I can't believe he would do that. Do you think we can talk him out of it?"

"I do. Harrington didn't get this far in life without being a shrewd businessman. Plus, deep down he doesn't want to hand you over. Once we explain to him, I think he'll see things our way. And if not... Well, you'll just have to subdue him, and we'll go on the run. Together."

"He might bring more guards with him."

"I don't think that would be a problem for you. But it could make things difficult. Hopefully, he shows up alone."

"Should we tie him up when he gets here so he'll have to listen?" Kate asked.

"I'd rather not. That will be a last resort. Harrington is a reasonable man, and he's well aware of your talents."

The doorbell rang.

Sitting at the kitchen table, Kaitlyn tensed, but her sensors quickly relaxed her muscles again.

"He's not alone. Two others are with him." Kaitlyn said.

Lucas leaned down and kissed her on the forehead. "It will be alright."

Wishful thinking, she thought as she followed Lucas's tall, athletic frame across the room. He turned and gave her a reassuring smile before he swung the door open.

"What's this..." Harrington stopped mid-sentence, his gaze stopped on Kaitlyn his eyes narrowed.

"Don't do anything rash. I know this looks bad, but give me a moment and I'll explain," Lucas said.

Harrington stepped through the door, not taking his eyes off his prized possession. Terry and Mirko stood on either side of him. They looked alert, but unsure what to do.

Lucas shut the door quickly behind them. Kaitlyn watched them closely, ready to spring into action if he became a threat.

"Lucas, what's going on here? You better have a good explanation why my billion dollar classified project is sitting in your kitchen, while I have my whole security force working round the clock searching for her."

"I asked you to come alone."

"And I told you—you work for me, not the other way around."

"With all due respect, I think everyone in this room knows the guards are no more than show. If Kaitlyn wanted, she could easily take all of us without breaking a sweat."

"Wait in the car." Harrington barked at the guards.

"Are you sure?" Terry asked.

"Go."

They turned and walked out of the house. Kaitlyn relaxed somewhat. She didn't want to hurt them.

"Have a seat, and I'll explain everything. Do you want some coffee?"

"No, I don't want any damn coffee," Harrington snapped. "And I'm not sitting down. I want you to tell me what the hell is going on."

"Kaitlyn came to me in hopes I could mediate. We have a proposition for you."

Harrington rolled his eyes. "You've got to be kidding me."

"I'm afraid I'm not," Lucas said grimly. "Kaitlyn does not wish to be sold off to be some killing machine. I think after you hear us out, you will agree it's to your advantage to keep Kate to yourself."

"Oh, she's Kate, now?" Harrington raised an eyebrow. "Well, go on, boy. Spit it out."

"I know this is going to be hard for you to believe, but even after the countless upgrades, Kaitlyn still has emotions," Lucas said. "She's not the mindless robot we took her to be. She is a real living person with her own thoughts and feelings. She didn't want to leave the compound, and she got scared that you were going to sell her off."

His eyes darted back to Kaitlyn. "She has emotions? How is that possible?"

"The human body is complex. We really shouldn't be too surprised."

"Well, I'm pretty damn surprised. She has shown no evidence of human emotions. She barely responds when someone acknowledges her."

Kaitlyn nodded. "I was afraid you would strip me even more than you already had. So I kept my thoughts and feelings to myself."

Harrington looked back at Lucas, clearly surprised. "And how would this be in my best interest? Why shouldn't I call a team to pick her up right now?"

"Kaitlyn has already proven she can escape from us, and we both know your security team wouldn't stand a chance. She could have gone off on her own and started a new life, but she came back because she wants to help."

Kaitlyn stood up and walked toward Harrington, who was still standing near the door. He took a step backwards, clearly uncomfortable. "My old life is gone. I know that, but I want to make this new life the best it can be with the situation I'm in. I have all of these upgrades that make me 'super human.' I don't want them to go to waste, but I also don't want to be controlled by others. I want to do the right thing, but not at the expense of my freedom."

"What we are offering is a partnership of sorts," Lucas said.

Harrington laughed. "You must be out of your mind. Need I remind you who controls this situation? You belong to me, sweetheart. One command from me and Kaitlyn will be shut down for good."

"That's very true. But you're not going to shut her down. You put all you had into her, and she's perfect, just like you wanted. Harrington, this is really in your best interest. It's either this or you lose her for good. We all know she is more to you then a science project."

"I don't have time for games. Tell me. What's your proposal?"

Lucas took a deep breath. "You keep Kaitlyn for IFICS. You hire her as an independent contractor, with wages and full benefits. Sure, you can loan her out to the defense department, but you never give them control. Think of how much more power you'll have. They will be groveling at your feet, and you won't have to beg them to let you stay apprised of her."

"I don't want to be just a weapon," Kaitlyn said firmly. "I want to be a solution,"

Harrington's eyes were distant as he considered the proposal. His fingers were shaped in a triangle which he tapped at his lips. "It is an interesting proposition."

"You wouldn't have to give up control." Lucas reminded him knowing control was something Harrington thrived on. "And you would be able to see all your hard work in action, not handed over to the government who wouldn't appreciate her the way we do."

"I do loath the idea of giving her away. Regardless of the money and the prestige."

"There's really not much prestige when she's a covert black ops solider. The only people that will know aren't exactly your esteemed colleagues. At least this way you could see first hand what she is able to accomplish."

"As much as I hate to admit it the idea is appealing. Are you sure she's not pulling the wool over our eyes? What if she just wants us to think she has emotions?"

Lucas glanced over at Kaitlyn. "I assure you her emotions are real. I've seen her cry."

"Tears? That's impossible."

"I thought so too, but we were wrong."

"You continue to astound me Kaitlyn." Harrington looked at her as if seeing her for the first time.

"Please, Dr. Harrington, I won't let you down. Just give me a chance."

Harrington met Kaitlyn's gaze. "Let's get one thing straight. If I agree to this, you works for me. You would follow all the rules and regulations same as all my other employees. There will be no special treatment."

Kate nodded. "I don't want special treatment."

"This would be highly classified and dangerous. You could get killed or sent to jail. All of us could go to jail. I would have to expand IFICS. We don't have the resources to run the kind of operation you're suggesting. What are the other demands? Clearly, that's not all?"

"I want to live off-compound," Kaitlyn spoke up, even though she hadn't discussed the concern with Lucas. "I'm sick of that tiny white room with its stupid lock."

Harrington nodded thoughtfully. "I'm sure that could be arranged *if* Lucas thinks you are up to it. It goes without saying that you have to keep your real identity under wraps." He walked over and sank wearily into the leather sofa. Lucas sat beside him, but Kate remained standing.

Lucas nodded. "She could stay with me. She still needs integration training. She's not quite ready to blend in yet."

"Also, I want to taste food again."

Lucas and Harrington both looked at her in surprise.

"What? I know it can be done. If I can smell, I should be able to taste."

"But you don't need to eat," Lucas said, puzzled.

"I can eat, and I might as well enjoy it when I

do. I really want to taste a Butterfinger."

"Butterfinger?" Lucas shook his head and smiled.

"Can you fix that, Lucas?" Harrington asked.

He scratched his head. "Sure, that's an easy fix. Just one I never would have thought would need doing."

"Anything else?" Harrington asked clearly resigned to the idea.

"Yes. I want one of these inside me." She picked up the iPhone on the end table.

"What do you mean?" Harrington smiled for the first time since walking through the front door.

"Why can't I have this fancy map already installed in me and be able to ask Siri to search info for me on the all-knowing Google?"

Lucas grinned. "That might take more work, and I'm pretty sure she's under copyright, but I'm sure we can figure it out."

"Also, I want to be able to see Quess."

"The Adams' granddaughter?" Harrington asked.

"Yes, she's my friend."

He scoffed and shook his head with disbelief. "So, you have…friends? Does everyone know you're…well…still human?"

"Just Quess. She figured it out on her own. She's very bright. She kept my secret for months."

"Okay. I guess that's fine. I didn't realize you

were friends. Hell, I didn't realize you had your own thoughts. Anything else?"

"That's all I can think of for now." Kaitlyn knitted her hands together behind her back and gave him a sideways look. "This seems too easy."

Harrington laughed, holding his palms to the ceiling. "I don't know what you mean."

Trust me," he continued, "this is going to be far from easy to pull off. Perhaps one of the most difficult projects I've taken on. Making you was one thing, but controlling how your 'gifts' are used, that's a different kind of power, a kind that comes with many complications."

"Why aren't you trying to bring me back to the compound?" Kaitlyn asked, suspicious. "You're taking this really well. Too well. I thought I would have to restrain you until you saw things our way."

Harrington sat back on the couch. "I've spent the last forty-eight hours worried how I was going to explain this to those self-righteous, military official talking heads. It's with great pleasure that I can now tell them all to shove it."

"Lucas thought you would see it that way, but I wasn't convinced."

"So you have had us fooled this whole time?" Harrington stared up at her, clearly impressed. "That's incredible."

"Boring is more like it."

Harrington laughed. "I can imagine it was. So

tell me more."

She wasn't sure where to start, but she knew it was vital to have Harrington on her side. "I still have a lot to re-learn. My brain has been scrambled. But I really want to make this work. I'm willing to do anything it takes. Just... please don't take away what I have left. I should warn you, if I think that you or anyone else will try to alter me again in any way that I do not approve of, I'm gone. My life has value, and I won't let you take that from me again."

Harrington didn't speak for a moment. "Understood. I wish I had known earlier."

"We can tweak things with the programming, but basically she will have to learn how to blend in to society. It will get easier with time," Lucas chimed in.

"Do you think it will interfere with her abilities?"

"No. I don't. I think it will only enhance her. She knows right from wrong and has a conscience. Her skills far surpass any soldier's, and she has a strong sense of morality and justice."

"Think of the possibilities. I don't know why I didn't think of this myself," Harrington muttered under his breath. "Kaitlyn, you realize you will have to complete any mission you are tasked with."

That gave her pause. "I'll be used for good?"

"It's not always so black and white. You may

have to do things you don't agree with."

Kate crossed her arms over her chest and looked at Lucas.

"It's always been that way for soldiers. Sometimes the black and white lines can blur to grey." Lucas said calmly.

Kaitlyn nodded her head, but she knew she would figure out a way to only do good.

"So it's settled." Harrington sprang to his feet. "We should get back to the lab right now and get started."

"Not so fast." Lucas held up a hand. "Kaitlyn should have at least one day to herself. We can start the upgrades tomorrow. I'm sure you have a lot of phone calls to make."

Harrington shoved his hands deep into his pockets. "You're right. Kaitlyn, I'm sorry. If we had known, I'm sure we would have done things differently."

"Thank you." Kaitlyn took his offered hand and shook it. "I was worried you were going to try to drag me back to the lab and throw away the key."

His face fell. "God, I feel like a jackass."

"As long as I have some freedom and can make a difference, that's enough for me."

"You will have some freedom Kaitlyn, but don't forget at the end of the day I am in charge. You work for me."

She nodded. She needed Harrington as much

as he needed her.

After seeing Harrington out, Lucas wrapped his arms around Kaitlyn with a grin. "A whole day off. What should we do?"

"We could spend the day in your bedroom." Kaitlyn tiptoed to kiss him.

"That does sound tempting. Why don't we spend the day out, and the evening in the bedroom? I want to show you off to the world."

Kaitlyn's face went blank. "What do you mean show me off?"

"Not that way, Kate. I want to show off my beautiful girlfriend. Meaning, I'm honored to have you by my side."

She glowed, squeezing his waist. "You make me feel beautiful."

"I was thinking we could go bowling, or to the movies. Go on a real date."

Kaitlyn thought it over, and then smiled. "I like that idea."

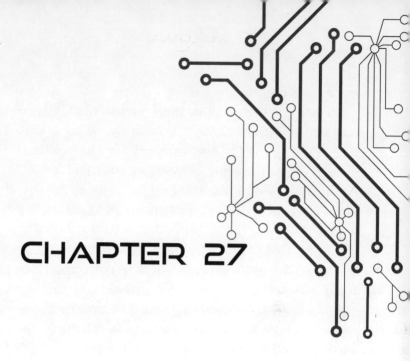

CHAPTER 27

"Are you sure this looks okay?" Kaitlyn asked, staring at herself in front of a mirror in the clothing shop.

From the chair in the waiting area, Lucas grinned. "You look great."

"I wish I knew what I liked." She was wearing jeans and a black sweater. The neck felt like it was choking her. Lucas said it was called a 'turtle neck,' which made sense. She had flicked through her internal encyclopedia and saw a plethora of turtles and their necks. But she was a person and not a turtle.

"I don't like the sweater," she said finally.

Lucas laughed. "See, you already know what you like. Or don't like, anyway. One minute. Let me grab a couple more. Don't move."

Lucas returned with three sweaters. "Do you like any of these?"

"This one." Kaitlyn reached for the charcoal v-neck, then moved to tug off her sweater.

Lucas grabbed her hand, speaking quietly. "Not here, Kate. You need to go in the dressing room."

"Oh, right Sorry, I forgot. All the time being observed by the cameras." Kaitlyn dropped her head and went back into the dressing room. She was so used to everything being recorded; it was going to take some time for her to adjust to the idea of privacy. Moments later, she came out with the sweater and jeans in her hands. "These will work. I guess I'll never be able to wear a dress again. At least not in public."

Lucas frowned and glanced around for eavesdroppers before he said, "We could always change the coating to look like skin."

"No. I like the reminder of knowing exactly what I am."

"You're unique."

Kate smiled. "I guess that's one way to put it."

"Do you want to keep shopping or finish later?"

"Later. I just wanted something to wear for our date. Shopping doesn't seem as fun as Quess makes it sound."

"I'm not much of a fan of shopping, myself." He kissed her gently, his thumbs brushing her jaw line. "You can change in the bathroom, and then we'll go on our first official date."

Lucas pulled into a bowling alley. "Heads up. I used to be on the bowling team. I figure I might actually have a chance of beating you at something for once." He gave her a crooked grin that made her heart skip a beat.

"I guess we'll see," she said smugly as she shut her car door and walked around to take his hand. "My visual-spatial awareness is quite excellent."

Competitiveness was ingrained in her, even before she had died. She'd been captain of the swim team for two years. She broke the tri-county meet record her junior year. Kaitlyn realized it was the first time she'd remembered that since her memories were unlocked, and it brought her a pang of sadness. Her parents had been at that meet. They'd been so proud of her.

Lucas glanced over at her. He stopped walking and tugged her around to face him. "What's wrong?"

Kaitlyn smiled sadly. "I was thinking about my parents."

He didn't say anything, but he wrapped his strong arms around her and held her tight for several moments.

When she was ready, they walked into the dimly lit building hand in hand. They were assailed by the smell of fried food and stale beer, and Kaitlyn stepped back as a tipsy brunette in high heels bumped into her. The girl balanced her clear plastic cup of beer and waved at Kate before she wandered off. "Sorry!"

"I'm going to get our shoes and lanes," Lucas told Kaitlyn, squeezing her hand before he let go. "I'll be right back."

Kaitlyn nodded and scanned the bowling alley. It was really loud. There were a lot of people inside, congregating on the hardwood of the lanes and wandering around the area near the bar. It made her uncomfortable.

She turned back to watch Lucas. A pretty blonde girl stood behind the counter, smiling at him. Kaitlyn narrowed her eyes as the girl threw back her head and laughed at something Lucas said.

Caution, flashed on her screen. Her body tensed, and she made her way to Lucas's side.

She snaked her arm around him and glared at the girl. Lucas patted her hand, and she relaxed somewhat, but kept her eyes glued to the blonde. The girl dropped the money as she handed it back to Lucas, and Kaitlyn registered her suddenly elevated heart rate; Kaitlyn had made her nervous. She wondered what made her mood change from laughter to a bundle of nerves so quickly. She must have done something wrong.

Lucas grabbed their shoes and pulled her with him. "What was that about, Kate?"

"She was potentially a threat."

"To who?" he asked wearily.

"I don't know. I got the caution flash."

Lucas groaned. "We're going to have to make some changes to your programming now that we know you have feelings. Could you have been jealous and saw her as a threat?"

Kaitlyn thought about the emotion jealousy and nodded. "It could have been. I didn't like the way she was laughing and smiling at you."

Lucas stopped in his tracks. "Listen, Kate. Emotions are not easy to deal with for anyone, and I think it might be more amplified with you. There is not a woman alive that will ever be a threat to you. You are all I want. Understand?"

"I'm trying to. It's just so confusing, Lucas."

He kissed her softly, and a sense of calm washed over her. For a moment, it was only them in the room, embracing beneath the dingy lights.

Lucas broke the kiss with a cocky grin. "Let's see if I have a chance at winning against you. I'm telling you, I was captain of the team. Well co-captain."

Lucas explained how the game worked. When it was Kaitlyn's first turn, she walked up to the lane and pulled back her arm, then expertly rolled the ball down the lane. She jumped up, grinning when it cracked loudly against the pins, sending them all flying. Strike.

Six turns later, she hit her sixth strike in a row. People were starting to notice.

"Kate." Lucas sidled up to her, shaking his head in amusement. "I know this idea will sound foreign to you, but you've got to miss some of the pins on your next turn."

"Why? This game is so easy."

"Blend in, remember?"

Kate looked around. People were watching her. "I can do that."

Lucas smiled. "I'll be back. I'm going to get a drink."

"Okay." Kate sat down on the hard plastic chair to wait for Lucas to return. She wondered if she was ever going to get anything right.

She felt a man approaching before she saw him, and WARNING flashed. He was six foot, one-ninety-five with dark hair; she couldn't make out his eye color in the dim light, but they were pale. Her body tensed, and she stood up, ready to spring into action.

"Well, hey there, pretty thing. You sure are putting on quite a show for the rest of us." He came to a stop only inches away.

Kaitlyn's alarms were off the charts. She stood with her feet shoulder-width apart, balancing on the balls of her toes in case she needed to act. But a small part of her remembered the earlier interaction with the blonde girl flashing *Caution*, and for the first time, she was uncertain. Was this guy a real threat?

"What do you want?" she asked calmly and wished Lucas would hurry up.

"I'm looking at it." His hand came forward as if he were going to touch her, and without considering whether she was doing the right thing, Kaitlyn grabbed his arm and threw him over her shoulder. He hit the hardwood floor hard on his back, and a long, low moan escaping him.

Lucas rushed up, his eyes wide as he leaned down to help the guy, who, winded, was struggling to get to his feet.

"What the hell happened?" Lucas asked, glaring at the man.

"He tried to touch me," Kate said, her voice flat. Now that she'd laid him out flat, her indicators had switched to not a threat.

"That's it?" Lucas groaned.

"Your girlfriend is a freak, man. I just wanted to say hello, that's all, and then she went all ninja on my ass." He rubbed the back of his head.

"I thought he was a threat," Kate mumbled.

"She doesn't like to be touched."

"No kidding."

"You need to leave." Lucas tilted his head towards the door.

"You're lucky I don't call the cops on her for

assault." The guy stalked off, his ego probably hurt more than his body.

Lucas closed his eyes and took a deep breath. "You're not ready, Kate. We need to get out of here. Now."

Panic coursed through her veins. She grabbed his arms. "Don't say that! I can get ready. I promise. Please don't make me go back." Her eyes glistened by the neon lights.

"We have a lot of work to do," he said gently. "As you are right now, you pose a danger to the population. We'll bring in help. Specialists. You need to relearn the rules of society."

"I can't go back there." Kaitlyn lowered her eyes. "I just can't. Not to live."

"Aw, Kate." Lucas put an arm around her shoulders and hugged her. "I would never make you move back there. You can still stay with me, but we can't have any more of these outings until we get some help."

"You promise I can stay with you?"

"I promise. But Kate, this is serious. If you do something bad, you could get taken away from me."

The seriousness of the situation hit her hard. "I'll learn, Lucas. I don't want to lose you. Whatever it takes, I'll do it."

"Let's get out of here." Lucas grabbed her hand, and they went back to the safety of his house, their first official date over.

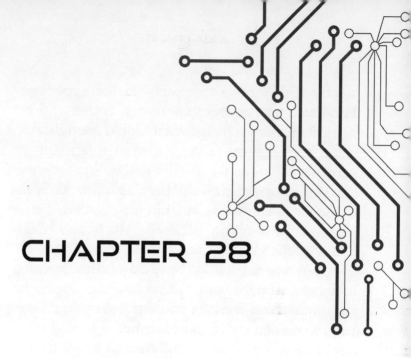

CHAPTER 28

SIX MONTHS LATER

Dr. Olivia Chambers looked up from behind her desk as Lucas walked into her office. She was an attractive woman in her late thirties with long, dark hair. Today, it was piled into a messy bun. "Good morning, Lucas."

"Thanks for seeing me."

"You know you're always welcome. I still think we should talk about setting up regular sessions." She leaned back in her plush leather chair and nodded to the seat across from her.

Lucas reluctantly sat down. He always felt uncomfortable around the doctor. She had an uncanny ability to see right through people.

He didn't bother to reply to her statement. They had gone over it many times before—Lucas had no interest in therapy. He'd had enough of it when he was younger after his father left. But he knew Dr. Chambers was vital to Kate's progress.

Her expertise was in treating patients with Aspergers. She was at the top of her field, Cognitive Behavioral Therapy. It was a field based on the idea that how we think, how we feel, and how we act are intertwined and all interact together. Specifically that our thoughts determined our feelings and our behavior. At the suggestion of a colleague, Harrington brought the doctor in to work with Kaitlyn, and already they had seen amazing changes. Kate was less anxious out in public, was learning to react reasonably to certain social cues, and overall seemed more at ease with herself.

Dr. Chambers had been instrumental in Kaitlyn's reintegration.

"Kate's made tremendous progress. It's quite remarkable really," Dr. Chambers said.

"Do you think she's ready? Harrington is itching to get her in the field." Lucas wasn't sure how much longer he could hold off Harrington. So much money had been dumped into the program getting it ready for Kaitlyn; all they needed now was for Kate to be ready to move the project forward.

"I think she's as ready as she can be, given

the circumstances. Pairing her with Erik was a brilliant idea. He will be sure to keep her in check." Dr. Chambers said, leaning back in her chair and folded her hands on her abdomen. "They make a great team."

Lucas felt a twinge of jealousy at the mention of Erik, even though he knew the pairing was the right thing to do. They needed someone with her at all times, and sadly Lucas did not have the skill-set to be her partner. Erik was a super-solider in his own right without any enhancements. A highly decorated former Marine Recon. Lucas knew the soldier would be able to handle any situation thrown their way; making sure Kate was able to do her job was Erik's main priority.

"Do I sense jealousy, Lucas?"

"I'll get over it." He wished it didn't bother him that the two spent so much time together, but that was required to form a partnership. They had to have each other's back. And it was Lucas that Kaitlyn went home with every night, he reminded himself.

Dr. Chambers smiled and didn't reply, which pissed Lucas off.

"So you are giving the go-ahead?"

"I am. I've already let Harrington know. As you can imagine, he's very pleased."

"I'm sure he is." Lucas tried to keep his apprehension off his face.

"She'll still need to see me on a regular basis. This is a long term solution."

"I know. Thank you for everything you've done. She really has made drastic improvements. Every day she seems a little more comfortable."

"You've been a huge factor in that as well, Lucas. You're her anchor."

"Anchor?"

"Yes, you keep her grounded." Dr. Chambers eyed him in her knowing way. "I really don't know if she could have done this without you."

"Thanks."

"It's the truth."

With a parting nod, Lucas stood up and walked out of the office. Dr. Chambers had said exactly what he needed to hear. She seemed to have a knack for that.

Lucas found his way to Harrington's office. The moment they had all been waiting for was finally here. He knew Kaitlyn was capable of doing whatever was required, but he would still be on edge until she returned from her first mission.

Behind the U-shaped desk in the outer office, the secretary smiled. "He's waiting for you."

Harrington grinned when Lucas walked in. "We've done it, Lucas!"

"That we have, sir," Lucas replied.

The man walked over from where he'd been gazing out the window and clapped a big hand to

Lucas's shoulder. "Keeping Kate for ourselves was a brilliant idea. We are going to be the envy of every organization out there."

"Let's not celebrate until we see how it goes."

Harrington waved him away. "I'm sure it will go smoothly."

"Famous last words." Lucas ran his hand through his hair, surprised to find it was shaking. "When will they leave?"

"They fly out in the morning. Six am. They'll touch down by noon our time."

"Will they be safe?" Lucas asked, using Harrington's 'they' even though he really only cared about Kate.

"We'll have eyes on them at all times," Harrington said.

At least that was something. He would go insane not knowing if Kate was okay.

Harrington slid a manila envelope across the table. "I'll let you do the honor."

Lucas hesitated, and then accepted the envelope. "Now or in the morning?"

"Why wait?" Harrington boomed. "Let her beautiful mind sleep on it and play out all possible scenarios."

"I'll bring it to them now," Lucas said calmly. Inside, he trembled.

This is it.

It was training time. Lucas found them in the combat room, and stood watching through the window as Kate and Erik stalked in a circle around each other. Erik moved forward swiftly, but Kate was faster. They were both so intent on each other it was as if they were lost in a dance that no one else was allowed access to.

Erik pivoted from his back foot to his front. He threw a flurry of punches, all which Kate blocked with ease.

Kate flipped through the air and locked her legs around Erik's throat dropping him to the ground. Erik somehow managed to get free and sprang back to his feet.

Lucas had seen enough. He couldn't watch them function so smoothly, so perfectly together—both powerful and deadly. He pushed through the door, but neither even glanced his way. Kate was aware he was in the room; she was programmed to know. But he wasn't a threat: Erik was.

A flurry of punches were exchanged, and next thing Lucas knew, Kaitlyn was splayed across Erik's body, and he was tapping out.

The sight of her body pressed against Erik's made Lucas's blood boil, but he closed his eyes and took a deep breath. He had to accept that Erik was part of her life now. He was also a lifeline, of sorts, for her.

Kaitlyn jumped up and walked towards Lucas. She was so alive; energy radiated off her. He wanted to wrap his arms around her, but they were at work.

Lucas held up the envelope. "You leave tomorrow."

"Really?" Kate's eyes danced with excitement.

Erik came closer, leaning his craggy face over Kaitlyn's shoulder. He certainly wasn't a handsome man, but his intensity seemed to draw women to him. Lucas had overheard the nurses talking about Erik on more than one occasion.

It bothered Lucas that Kate didn't mind the Marine in her personal space.

"Where are we going?" Erik asked gruffly.

Lucas shrugged. "It's all in there. I'll leave you two to go over the details."

Kaitlyn looked like she was about to explode with excitement. She bounced on the tips of her toes and clutched the envelope to her chest. "Thank you, Lucas. For believing in me."

"I will always believe in you," he said softly, but she had already turned to open the envelope with her partner.

Lucas left the room, his heart aching. He really needed to get his jealousy in check.

Kaitlyn laid her head on Lucas's shoulder, breathing in his musky scent. There was a time she had thought happiness was impossible for her, but she had been wrong. Life was better than she could have ever hoped. She had come to terms with her past and looked forward to the future. She still missed her parents, but she felt it was best they thought she was gone.

Lucas ran his hands through her hair and pressed a kiss to her forehead. "I'll be worried about you."

"Don't be. You know I can take care of myself, and Erik will be there."

"Right. Erik."

Kaitlyn stared at Lucas, his face bathed in the moonlight that filtered through the curtains. His dark hair curled at the nape of his neck, and his strong jawbone drew her closer. She lightly kissed her way from the tip of his ear down his jaw and made her way eagerly to his full warm lips.

"Croatia is so far away." Lucas said softly as he traced his finger around the plastic coating on her arm.

"You saw the file. Human trafficking. All those young girls sold into slavery," Kaitlyn said disgusted.

"He's a monster, and he has to be stopped." Lucas agreed.

"I'll finally be able to use these skills for good."

Lucas turned to his side, his face serious. "Kate. I need to tell you something."

"Yes?" She propped herself on her elbow and stared down at him.

"I'm in love with you, Kate." The words came out in a rush. "I love you so much. The thought of losing you is like a weight crushing my chest."

She smiled, pushed him back, and climbed on top of him. "I know you love me, Lucas." She pressed her lips to his and ran her hands along his muscular chest. She could never get enough of him. Being so close, skin to skin, drove her completely crazy.

"You know?" he asked, smiling against her lips. "I've wanted to say the words for months. I didn't think you were ready."

She leaned down and whispered in his ear. "I love you, too."

"You do? Are you sure?" He gripped her by her arms and pushed her back so he could look her in the eye. "You don't have to say it back just because I said it first. I just wanted you to know. In case anything happened on the mission."

"I feel like I've always loved you. I thought that was obvious?"

Lucas smiled. "I guess I needed to hear it out loud."

"I love you, Lucas. Should I say it again?"

Lucas wrapped his arms around her, rolling her beneath him. "Maybe one more time."

To Be Continued

Acknowledgments

A special thanks to my family for putting up with me while I write.

I would also like to thank Heather Adkins, Claire Teeter, and Sarah Billington for their editing skills, and Mayme and Lisa Markson for beta reading, all of whom make this book readable.

Eden Crane for the amazing cover.

My assistant, Allison Porter, who holds everything together.

My husband for his technical and tactical knowledge.

My fans for all your support which means more then you will ever know.

And the Bloggers who help spread the word—without you, I wouldn'thave made it this far. Thank you!!!

Also by Julia Crane

About the Author

Julia Crane is the author of the YA paranormal fiction novels: *Keegan's Chronicles*, *Mesmerized*, and *Eternal Youth*. Julia was greatly encouraged by her mother to read and use her imagination, and she's believed in magical creatures since the day her grandmother first told her an Irish tale. Julia has traveled far and wide to all the places her grandmother told her about, gaining inspiration from her journeys to places like Nepal, Cyprus, Sri Lanka, Italy, France and many more. And who knows? Maybe the magical creatures she writes about are people she met along the way.

Julia has a bachelor's degree in criminal justice. Although she's spent most of her life on the US east coast, she currently lives in Dubai with her husband and three children.

Find Julia online at juliacraneauthor.com

Interested in receiving updates on Julia's books? Join her mailing list! She'll only email about her books and will never share your information with anyone.

Word-of-mouth is crucial for any author to succeed. If you enjoyed *Freak of Nature*, please consider leaving a review where you purchased it. It would be greatly appreciated!

Made in the USA
Lexington, KY
06 April 2014